Sleaze Castle: The Director's Cut Part #0

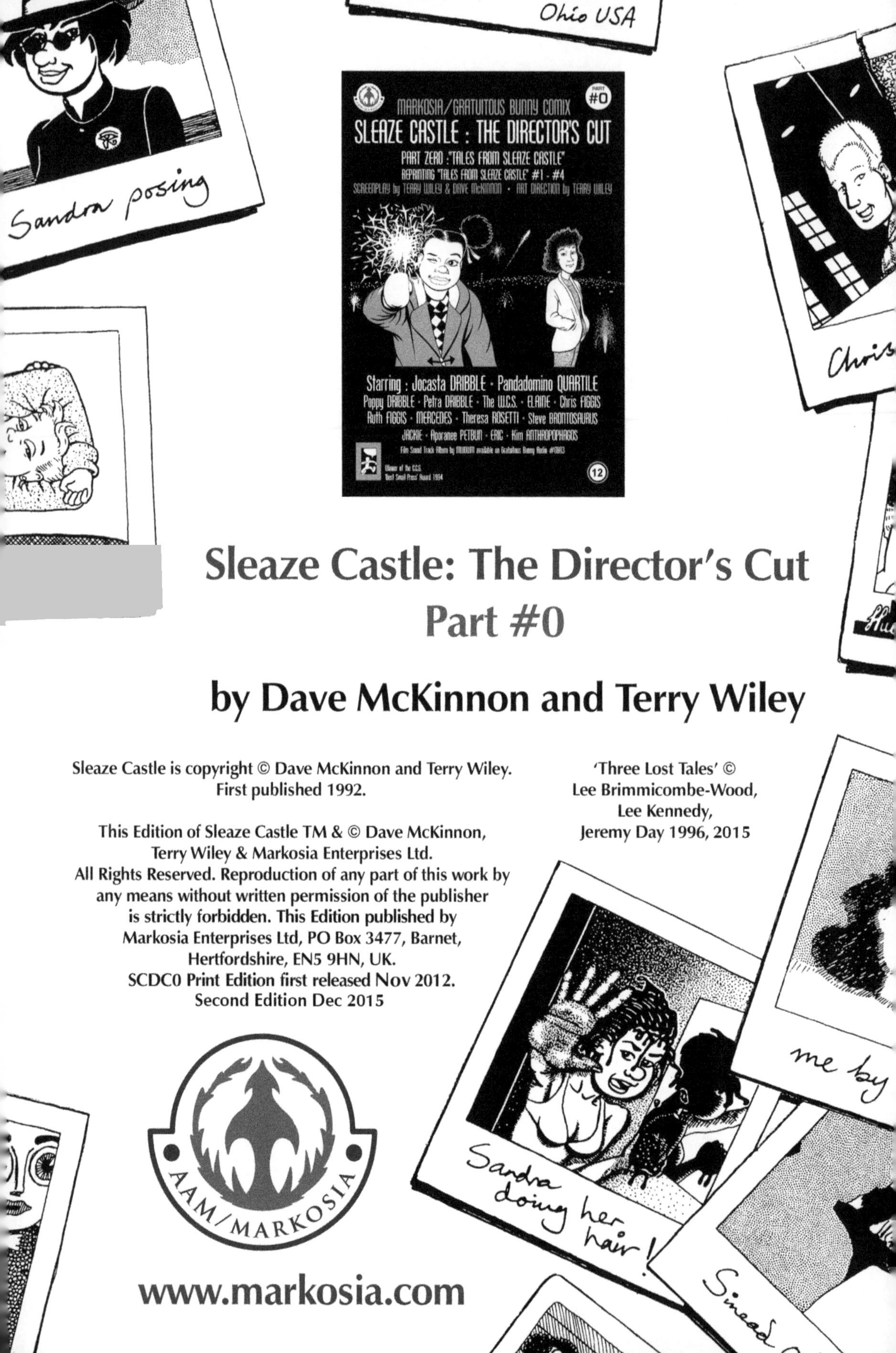

Sleaze Castle: The Director's Cut
Part #0

by Dave McKinnon and Terry Wiley

 This Edition published by Markosia Enterprises Ltd, PO Box 3477, Barnet, Hertfordshire, EN5 9HN, UK.
SCDC0 Print Edition first released Nov 2012.
Second Edition Dec 2015

www.markosia.com

Introduction to the new Director's Cut print editions

It seems like no time since I was writing introductions to digital editions of *Sleaze Castle* – that new-fangled futuristic science-fiction format! That's a far cry from the non-word processed, badly printed (complete with wandering cover colours), world we were working in when we started the series. They've now been available for some time; for iPad, Kindle, and other tablets. We've also had a bumper printed volume of the full run.

Perhaps, all these years on, these are now something of a historical curiosity – some of the first 'graphic novels' to come out of the British indie small press. It is a little frightening to realise that the earliest material in these volumes is almost literally from half a lifetime ago - written as it was, when we were in our mid 20's. I'm now 50 (Terry is EVEN OLDER!). The most recent material is from a little over a decade ago, and these introductions (overdue, as usual) are the only contribution to the comics medium that I have made since then. As usual, Terry has done all the work for this (including newly reworked covers) - and I've done very little. (The new covers were my idea, though).

Newcomers will notice a lot of variation in quality (in writing and artwork) as you go through the series... remember, though, that the bits of the story that are chronologically first are NOT those that we created first. Hopefully what you'll experience will be a progressive improvement in quality. When we started, we honestly didn't know what we were doing (see above for evidence of this in our choice of printer!) - being propelled only by Dave Sim's "just publish it yourself"-style philosophy. I think it was several issues before we really made contact with other indie small-press creators. Looking back, I'm not entirely certain what the spark was that actually made us start - or what shaped the storyline(s). I remember wanting a big castle (shades of *Gormenghast*), and stuff to do with dimensions and parallel universes. We had a female lead (Jo) almost on a whim, and then the character who became Panda was made female because we thought it best to have them both as the same gender. I don't think that *Love and Rockets* (which we were both reading around then) influenced us in this decision. Certainly Jo and Panda are nothing like Hopey and Maggie, and I can't say that I had any real interest in specifically portraying female characters, or profess to having any insight into them (then or now). Its hard to now imagine that they could be other than they are and - given the level of female readership that we picked up, we seemed to have done OK.

DaveMcK Nov 2012

ANOTHER EARTH

ANOTHER DIMENSION

Another reason to go *shopping*...

... ZE LINK VILL COMMENCE IN 55 ZEKONDS- -ARE YOU READY ?
ABSOLUTELY! I CAN'T WAIT TO GET OUT OF THIS PILE
-BUT MA'AM - THERE ARE STILL TWO IMPORTANT RITUALS WHICH REQUIRE MA'AM'S PRESENCE
OH, FOR PITY'S SAKE, -I'LL ONLY BE GONE TEN MINUTES OUR TIME...

MA'AM, THEY'RE OVERDUE - THE ARCHIVAL CALENDAR CLEARLY STATES-
OH SHUT UP!-
WHOOF - THAT'S A HEAVY ONE!
TEN KILOGRAMS EXACTLY, MA'AM
TEN ? I'VE STILL GOT CHANGE LEFT OVER FROM THAT SEVEN I TOOK LAST TIME!
...OH WELL, WHY NOT...

I MUST PROTEST, MA'AM- -THIS BEHAVIOUR IS NOT IN KEEPING WITH THE RECORD OF MA'AM'S ROYAL PRECEDENTS...
ANY ZEKOND NOW...
GAH!! WHOSE PLANET IS IT ANYWAY?!
-I'LL DEAL WITH IT- -IF I FEEL LIKE IT- -LATER, OKAY ?
-BE SEEING YOU...

PROLOGUE

"...It's late September, and I really should be back at school..."

LOOKS LIKE YOU'RE ESCAPING JUST IN TIME. IF HE TURNS UP AGAIN I'LL TELL HIM YOU'VE MOVED INTO A COMMUNE WITH AN ICELANDIC LION TAMER OR SOMETHING.
GOOD ONE.
PENBAG
* sigh * THIS LOT'S NEVER GOING TO FIT INTO ONE TRUNK AND ONE BAG. WHAT DO I NOT ACTUALLY NEED THIS TERM ??
-YOU COULD TRY LEAVING SOME OF THE MENAGERIE BEHIND!...
PENBAG
...HONESTLY, JO! THE AMOUNT OF TOYS YOU HAVE AT YOUR AGE IS TOTALLY OFFSKI!!
THEY'RE NOT ALL TOYS! SOME OF THEM ARE...RESEARCH. TV SPINOFFS AND SUCH. PART OF MY THESIS.
WELL, YOU DON'T NEED FOZZIE, OR BONZO, OR THE CLINGY KOALA- -THERE! ROOM FOR SOME MORE IMPORTANT STUFF.
I SUPPOSE SO.
COULD YOU PASS ME THOSE FILES, PETRA?
O.K...
HEY!!! THAT'S MY TINY TELLY! YOU CAN'T TAKE THAT!
OH, PLEEASE, PETRA! I HAVE TO HAVE IT TO CATCH "TAKE THE HIGH ROAD" - THE NEXT EPISODE'S ON WHILE I'M ON THE TRAIN AND I'LL MISS IT!
NO FEAR! IT WAS MY 18TH BIRTHDAY PRESENT!

AWWW, PET-RAAAHH! IT'S A SOAP! THEY DON'T REPEAT SOAPS – I'LL HAVE A GAP IN MY SUMMER PROJECT AND LOSE A GRADE!
TOUGH!
– IT'S YOUR OWN DAMN FAULT FOR TAKING SUCH A CANDY-FLOSS SUBJECT ALL THE WAY TO M.A LEVEL!
GIMME MY TELLY!
MEANWHILE, DOWNSTAIRS...
BUMP!
THUD!
CRASH!
?
SCARPE
BIP
CIAO!
LA PRINCIPESSA DIANA: DIETRO LE TENDE
YOU HARDLY EVER EVEN WATCH IT!
THAT'S 'COS YOU'RE ALWAYS WATCHING IT IN THE BATH OR SOMETHING!
THUMP THUMP THUMP THUM THUM
WHAT ON EARTH IS ALL THIS SHOUTING AND BANGING?
JO'S GOING TO PINCH MY TELLY FOR THREE WHOLE MONTHS!
I NEED THE WATCHMAN TELLY FOR MY COURSE AND PETRA WON'T LEND ME IT!
CALM DOWN, THE PAIR OF YOU!
...OHH, IF ONLY I'D THOUGHT ABOUT IT MORE, I'D HAVE BOUGHT THE TELLY FOR JO'S TWENTY-FIRST AND GIVEN YOU SOMETHING ELSE!
hmmm.
WELL I THINK IT SHOULD GO TO WHOEVER USES IT MOST. FAIR? O.K. LADIES...
...WHO WATCHES THE WATCHMAN?
we know!

• Sep. '86 : Castaway

Interplanetary Trade

101

The Gold Standard.

1.1: Export

1.2: Import !
?
HMM... COULD DO WITH MERCEDES ...
ZIP
TUM TE TUM... ...PYRAMID'S ONLY £25.99...
!?
WOBBLE
CLATTER
SHUDDER
RUMBLE
CLATTER
RATTLE
JIGGLE
FIRE EXIT
STAFF ONLY
EEEK!
SYDNEY

KINGS
THEATRE
STAGE DOOR
DRESSING ROOM
KNOCK
KNOCK
COME IN!...
LEE! THE DOOR IN FINNEX IS GONE!!!
WHAT??
– I OPENED THE DOOR AND IT WAS JUST A CUPBOARD!!!
GONE?... – LOOK JUST CALM DOWN A SECOND WHILE I CHECK ON THE RADIO...

HELLO PROF- DO YOU READ ME ?!
AH LEE! DOUBTLESS YOU HAF NOTICED ZAT ZER PORTAL HAS GONE.
ANY IDEA WHAT'S CAUSED IT ?
VELL, IT ZEEMZ A MOZT UNPRECEDENTED TIME DIZTURBANCE BROKE ZER SPACE-TIME LINKS UND DAMAGED ZER EQUIPMENT ALZO – ENOUGH FUNKTION REMAINED FOR ME TO RE-ESTABLISH ZER ZEITLICHVERBINDUNG VIZ TERRA, BUT ZER PORTAL HAS APPEARED 2317 METRES NORTHVEST... ... UND 178 DAYZ AHEAD OF YOUR PRESENT LOCATION!!
178 – WHAT? DO YOU MEAN I'M STUCK HERE FOR SIX MONTHS?!
I'M AFRAID ZO- -HOWEVER, I SHALL CALL YOU BACK IN A FEW MINUTEZ VEN YOU ARRIVE!
UGGHH!... – THIS IS A NICE PLACE TO VISIT, BUT I DON'T FANCY LIVING HERE!!
NOW NOW! DON'T BE SUCH A BIGOT- -EARTH'S VERY NICE ONCE YOU GET USED TO IT.
OHHH...... BUGGER!
WELLL, I S'POSE THIS'LL HAVE TO GO- -I WOULD STICK OUT A MILE WITH THIS COLOURATION.
AT LEAST YOU WON'T HAVE TO WORRY ABOUT HAIR DYE AND MAKEUP- - I CAN GET YOU MASSES OF IT ROUND HERE.
LENNY LILO
HEY – I HOPE YOU HAVEN'T SPENT ALL YOUR U.K. CURRENCY FROM THIS TRIP!
NO, LUCKILY, ENOUGH – THERE'S AT LEAST 9½ 'K' LEFT... – OH, HERE WE GO...
BUZZ BUZZ BUZZ
HI, PANDA... ... THIS IS PANDA!!
err.... HELLO?
NOW, DON'T WORRY- – IT WAS A BIT FRAUGHT TO BEGIN WITH, BUT IT GOT BETTER LATER ON! WRITE THIS DOWN...
FIRST, YOU HAVE TO POSE AS A STUDENT- -THAT'S IN ORDER TO BE IN THE RIGHT PLACE AT THE RIGHT TIME – BUT YOU'LL ALSO MEET THIS DIPPY GIRL CALLED JO...
– BUT MEANWHILE, I'VE JUST GOT BACK, I'M KNACKERED, AND I NEED A LONG HOT BATH! I'LL EXPLAIN MORE DETAILS LATER ON – BE SEEING YOU!
HOW STRANGE!
A STUDENT? AM I HAVING ME ON?
– OH WELL – – IF I CAN'T TRUST ME, WHO ELSE CAN I TRUST?!
!

Autopilot 11.23

SCHOOLY... BLUE REMEMBERED HILLS (DENNIS POTTER, COLIN JEAVONS, JANINE DUVITSKI ETCETERA)... ..."A SHROPSHIRE LAD", A.E. HOUSMAN... HOW'S IT GOING MAN...
WHAT? HEY! THAT'S WHATSER-NAME...
!
TRUNDLE RATTLE
♩ HEY JO, WHERE'YOU GOING WITH THAT GUN IN YOUR - EH? ♩
HEY YOU! DON'T I KNOW YOU FROM SOMEPLACE?
ERM - I DON'T THINK SO.
SURE I DO- LEMME THINK... MUSTA BEEN YEARS AGO... HMM...
...ABOUT THE ONLY THING I REMEMBER FOR SURE IS, THE LAST TIME I SAW YOU, YOU WAS ABOUT 11 MONTHS PREGNANT, SITTING IN A SUNLOUNGER WITH A STRAW HAT AND MIRRORSHADES ON!
WHAT?!
...I'M AFRAID YOU'VE GOT THE WRONG PERSON ENTIRELY! I'VE NEVER EVEN... BEEN PREGNANT FOR A START!!
WELL I'LL BE... COULDA SWORE IT WAS YOU!
SORRY TO BOTHER YA- - US OLD UN'S GET CONFUSED AT OUR AGE!...
GOOD-BYE!
"OUR" AGE? - ABOUT EIGHT AND A HALF, LOOKING AT HER!
...THE CHEEKY LITTLE BITCH! ...KIDS THESE DAYS... ...SHOULD BE IN SCHOOL ANYWAY... "MUST HAVE BEEN YEARS"...
-SHE HARDLY HAD ANY TO SPREAD AROUND!
♪ 'ROUND ROUND, SPREAD AROUND, I SPREAD AROUND ♪ ...
-MIGHT HAVE BEEN A DERANGED DWARF?...
...MUST BUY SOME PEANUT BUTTER.
KUHLUNK TRUNDLE
Etc!

• Mission Improbable
Later That Same Evening . . .
HELLO? AM I THERE?
WHO'S SPEAKING, PLEASE?
. . . down in the Chaise Longue Room of Panda's apartments
OH, HAR HAR! I HEARD THAT ONE BEFORE- - IN FACT I REMEMBER SAYING JUST THAT ABOUT 6 MONTHS AGO!
OH YEAH? LOOK- YOU TOOK YOUR TIME — LEE'S DONE A WHOLE EVENING PERFORMANCE- - DID YOU ENJOY YOUR BATH?
YES, LOVELY! SORRY ABOUT THAT - I KEPT ME WAITING TOO.
YEAH, YEAH- JUST GET ON WITH IT...
Esta cerdita fue al mercado...
TUT TUT! EDGY, AREN'T WE? THIS'LL CURE YOUR SHOPPING ADDICTION - I DON'T INTEND MAKING ANOTHER ONE OF THOSE TRIPS FOR A WHILE...
... IN FACT, I THINK I'LL GO IN THE FRIDGE FOR ABOUT A YEAR TO RECOVER !...
?
FRAULEIN— YOU HAF CHANGED YOUR HAIR.
HOLD ON A SEC- THE PROF'S LOST HIS MARBLES AGAIN—
YES- MY HAIR'S DIFFERENT- I'VE BEEN STUCK ON EARTH FOR SIX MONTHS — REMEMBER?
er- NEIN
OH LORD!
WHAT'S UP?
...y esta cerdita se quedo en casa...
WHO IZ ZAT ON ZER RADIO?
ME.
YOU? HOW YOU?
?
ME! STUCK - BACK- -ON-EARTH!! - I COULDN'T GET BACK FOR SIX MONTHS 'COS YOU HAD A PROBLEM WITH THE PORTAL- -YOU DON'T REMEMBER?

???
ER... NEIN... GOINK I MUZT UND ON ZIS BE ZINKING...
FINE— -I'LL HANDLE IT. I'VE BEEN THROUGH ALL THIS ONCE ALREADY!
YOU HAF? AH GÜT...
oh dear... oh dear...
WHAT'S GOING ON?
RELAX - YOU'LL FIND OUT IN TIME. -NOW LISTEN- THIS IS WHAT YOU'VE GOT TO DO...
Esta cerdita comió rosbif...
FIRST UP— -GET YOUR HAIR COLOURED BLACK AND GET SOME MAKEUP ON THAT WHITE HIDE OF YOURS -LEE'LL HELP. IT'S A GOOD JOB YOU'VE GOT THOSE COLOURED CONTACT LENSES WITH YOU....
?
NEXT, YOU'LL NEED A BUNCH OF PASSPORT PHOTOS....
...USE THE MACHINES IN THE STATION— THAT'S THE ONLY PLACE OPEN AT THIS HOUR.
FUT
FAZN RUBJUBNUB BAGGLEPAP MOLEEDS!
YUCK!
YEUCH! NO WAY!
THESE WILL HAVE TO DO, I SUPPOSE...
...WHAT IS A PASSPORT ANYWAY?
YA FIGN FORRIN BAZA KAMN EAR WA YI FORRIN MOLEEDS!
HA HA! YOU'LL LOVE THIS BIT- YOU AND LEE ARE GOING TO BREAK INTO THE UNIVERSITY HOUSING OFFICE...
I SUPPOSE WE CAN NOW ADD BREAKING AND ENTERING TO YOUR CRIMINAL RECORD TO GO ALONG WITH YOUR DREADFUL ACTING!
HUH!
CRACK PRISE PRY!
...YOU'LL HAVE TO GET ROOM 144 IN ETHEL MERMAN HALL. YOU'LL HAVE TO DISPLACE THE POOR GIRL WHO SHOULD BE GOING IN THERE. -SHE'S A FIRST YEAR SO IT'LL PROBABLY BE PUT DOWN TO AN ADMINISTRATIVE ERROR...
GOT IT.

...THE PORTAL WILL APPEAR IN ROOM 143 FOR A FEW MOMENTS ONLY - PROF. HEAPS COULDN'T MAINTAIN IT FOR LONG, WITH IT BEING IN THE WRONG TIMEFRAME, I THINK. I WASN'T- YOU WON'T BE ABLE TO LIVE IN THAT ROOM 'COS THE GIRL IN THERE'S A SECOND YEAR POSTGRAD.-NO WAY WOULD THEY MIX UP HER ROOM AFTER FOUR YEARS...
RUB RUB
'SANDRA' - 'PANDA' - THAT'S GOOD...
'CASTLE'... WHY NOT...
SANDRA CASTL 144
GENER STUDIES
THIS FORM WANTS MY AGE - WHAT'S THE AGE OF A FIRST YEAR STUDENT AROUND HERE ?
ABOUT EIGHTEEN OR NINETEEN...
...EXACTLY HOW OLD ARE YOU ANYWAY?
NEVER ASK A LADY HER AGE! LET'S JUST SAY I'M QUITE A MATURE STUDENT, EH?
...ONCE YOU'VE FIXED UP SOME CONVINCING PAPERWORK, YOU'LL NEED PHOTOCOPIES OF IT BEFORE YOU SWAP IT FOR THE ORIGINALS...
IT KEEPS SAYING 'ERROR E5'
GURN!
WHIZZ!
"PAPER CRASH"?
OH YES - THIS IS IMPORTANT. WATCH OUT WHEN YOU'RE LEAVING - THERE'LL BE A SECURITY PATROL GOING BY JUST ABOUT THEN...
!
...YOU'LL NEED TO PUT THE COPIES OF THE FORMS AND STUFF INTO THE OFFICES OF THE HALLS OF RESIDENCE TOO...
gra...mmm...
...HALL card please...
...nhg... can't bring that LITTER BIN in here...snork...

RIGHT- -HAVING EXCHANGED ALL REFERENCES TO THE UNFORTUNATE Ms CARTER WITH YOUR OWN BOGUS CREDENTIALS, THAT SHOULD BE ABOUT IT FOR THE NIGHT.
- IT'LL BE AROUND FOUR THIRTY BY THEN- -GET SOME REST DOWN AT LEE'S PLACE...
...YOU'VE GOT A LOT OF SHOPPING TO DO BEFORE PRESENTING YOURSELF AT THE HALLS-
-YOU'LL BE EARLY, BY THE WAY, SINCE ALL THE OTHER NEWCOMERS WILL BE ARRIVING IN A FEW DAY'S TIME.
ANYTHING ELSE I SHOULD KNOW?
OH, LOADS- BUT I DIDN'T TELL ME BACK THEN, WHEN I WAS YOU, SO I'M NOT GOING TO TELL YOU NOW!...
...OH - DON'T DRINK THE WATER; TRY NOT TO WATCH TOO MUCH TELEVISION- THAT JOCASTA'S A REAL ADDICT...
...y esta cerdita comió nada...
...WATCH OUT FOR ALL THOSE CHICKEN MEALS - AND EAT LOTS OF PIZZA - YOU'LL LOVE IT.
- AND THAT'S ALL THERE IS TO IT! HAVE FUN, AND I'LL SEE YOU IN SIX MONTHS-
OH- NO, I WON'T, WILL I?
TA TA!
CLICK
AAAAAIIIII!
HAHAHAHA- STOP IT- HA HA HA HA HA HA
-PERO ESTA CERDITA DIJO UI UI UI! HASTA LLEGÓ A CASA!!
TICKLE TICKLE TICKLE
REALLY, MERCEDES! - IF IT WASN'T SO HARD TO GET STAFF, I'D SACK YOU!!
NO COMPRENDO UNA PALABRA SOLA DE INGLÉS, DOÑA.
sigh CON ESO BASTA, MERCEDES.
SUS DESEOS SON ORDENES PARA MI, DOÑA.
KLIK
Soon
...SANDRA CASTLE - -HERE FOR MY FIRST YEAR- -AND HERE'S MY LETTER OF ACCEPTANCE.
HALL CARD, MISS!
PETER GABRIEL SAYS "CON-DOM"
...YOU ARE A FEW DAYS EARLY YOU KNOW?
YA- ALL PART OF THE PLAN...
ETHEL MERMAN HALL /2
133 LORNA H TRISTERO
134 ALICE PORTILLO
135 SIMON MOON
136 LYDIA DIETZ
137 KATE LEMMON
138 LOUISE BALTIMORE
139 MARTHA DYMPSTOCK
140 DANA CARVEY
141 MIKE MYERS
142 KIM ANDROKLIDOS

Hey Jo : 2 Days Later

ERM? "FRESHER'S WEEK?"
FOR THE FIRST-YEARS - - THEY PUT ON DISCOS AND STUFF.
MOST OF THEM SHOULD ARRIVE TODAY.
?
AH, WELL... I'M FROM - err - - THAILAND (?) - MY DAD LIVES OUT THERE - AND THE FLIGHT OVER HERE MEANT I HAD TO COME EARLY.
BETTER CHANGE SUBJECT...
ERM... HASN'T IT BEEN QUIET AROUND HERE?
WELL, THAT'LL CHANGE FROM TODAY! I'M GOING INTO TOWN TO AVOID IT ALL - YOU WANT TO COME? I COULD SHOW YOU ABOUT.
O.K. - THANKS.
- sniff - ... I'VE GOT TO OPEN A BANK ACCOUNT ANYWAY - sniff - ... SO I'LL DO THAT... - sniff - ... TODAY... ... WHUPS...
HAAAAA
SHISHIM!
OOOH! OUCH!
WHAT'S WRONG?
CONTACT LENS!!
DON'T MOVE! YOU MIGHT STAND ON IT!
?
I'LL LOOK...
WHOO!
GOT IT IN ONE!
- WISH IT WAS ALWAYS THIS EASY!
TRUNDLE
GRIP!
RIGHT- ONCE YOU'VE PUT YOUR EYE BACK IN, YOU COULD GO AND GET YOUR THINGS - I'LL MEET YOU DOWN BY THE MAIN DOOR IN 10 MINUTES.
ALL RIGHT THEN!
- YERG! HATE DOING THIS...
SHH SHH
THAT WAS CLOSE!

ALL READY TO GO? LOOKS LIKE THEY'RE JUST BEGINNING TO GET IN
HMM.
UH-OH – SEEMS LIKE THERE'S BEEN ANOTHER COCKUP...
PLEEEZE LOOK AGAIN- CARTER – SANDRA CARTER. LOOK – HERE'S MY LETTER TO SAY I'VE GOT A PLACE...
C...C... CARTER, -MARK...
CARTWRIGHT, ANGELA...
CASTLE, SANDRA...
NOPE- SORRY YOU'RE NOT ON THE LIST...
THE LUMPY MEN
OCT 31
S.A.C.
SO WHAT ARE YOU DOING HERE?
I'M A POST-GRADUATE IN TELEVISUAL STUDIES – I WATCH A LOT OF T.V. AND FILMS.
...NOW, AS A POSTGRAD, I COULD HAVE A FLAT AS A SUB WARDEN...
WHAT'S THAT?
...THEY GET A FLAT IN THE HALLS OF RESIDENCE – -BUT, THEY'VE GOT TO TAKE TURNS TO STAY UP ALL NIGHT IN CASE THERE'S TROUBLE...
-AND BE A KILLJOY TO ANYONE WANTING A GOOD TIME. I COULDN'T BE BOTHERED WITH ALL THE HASSLE, SO I'M JUST IN AN ORDINARY ROOM LIKE YOU.
I SEE.
HMMM... ...I'M AFRAID THIS BRITISH WEATHER'S NOT AT ALL WHAT YOU'D BE USED TO.
OH I DON'T KNOW, IT'S A BIT CLOUDY, BUT –
RECLAIM DIDCOT
BABS
INERTIA MAKES THE WORLD GO ROUND
EEEK!
WHAT IS IT?
JO... WHAT THE HELL HAS HAPPENED TO THE SUN!?
OH, THAT...
...IT'S JUST A PARTIAL ECLIPSE- I HEARD IT WAS DUE.
...MOON IN FRONT OF SUN AND ALL THAT!
MOON! OF COURSE- I COMPLETELY FORGOT ABOUT IT...
SURELY THEY HAVE ECLIPSES IN THAILAND AS WELL?
YEAHHH.... ...BUT IT RAINS A LOT TOO... I MUST HAVE MISSED THEM ALL...

... SO, WHAT DOES YOUR DAD DO OUT THERE?
... OH, HE'S AN INTERNATIONAL DRUGS SMUGGLER.
KOFF! Really??
MAYBE...
HE HE HE HE
LATER
Midwest Barcloyd
... THIS IS THE ONE I'M WITH - BUT YOU CAN PICK WHICHEVER TAKES YOUR FANCY - THEY ALL SEEM TO INVEST IN DODGY REGIMES ABROAD...
... WOULD YOU SAY THAILAND HAS A DODGY REGIME??
7%
NEVER MIND - THIS ONE'LL DO...
WELL... URM... ER...
I ONLY ASKED!
INSIDE
STUDENTS! JOIN OUR
... AND SO, WHEN YOU DEPOSIT YOUR GRANT CHEQUE... WE'LL GIVE YOU TEN POUNDS... AND AN ALBUM TOKEN!...
WELL, ACTUALLY, I'M SELF FINANCING - - DADDY'S PRETTY RICH...
SYLVIA H. STEPFORD
GAK!
THERE YOU GO - NINE THOUSAND ONE HUNDRED POUNDS!
... DRUGS SMUGGLER, EH?
MM-HMM...
GOUGH'S VAN
Drive
551089
O.K. AL - WHAT DOES ZIGGY SAY I HAVE TO DO THIS TIME?
... SO, WHAT'RE YOU GOING TO USE THAT RECORD TOKEN ON?
... JIMI HENDRIX?
COMING SOON ★ THIN SPIRAL TARGETS STONE POSIES
NEW IN SLOVENIAN NAZI MUSIC
FREE CRYING MORRISSEY DOLL WITH LATEST LP
LPS WILL NOT BE PHASED OUT - OFFICIAL

8.27p.m.: ♪Sisters, Sisters...♪
I'LL GET IT, MAMA.
BRINGG BRINGG
BRINGG BRINGG
GRAZIE, LOVE.
5552369?
HI, PET-IT'S ME
HI SIS-WADDYA WANT-SCUM!
JUST CALLING TO SAY I'M ALL RIGHT -CREEP!
MAMA! IT'S JO--SAYS SHE'S ARRIVED O.K.
RIGHTO. I'M A BIT BUSY, SO I CAN'T COME DOWN.
MAMA SAYS SHE CAN'T COME TO THE PHONE -ZEEB!
THAT'S OK, I HAVEN'T MUCH CHANGE ANYWAY -BIMBO!
AIRHEAD!
BRUCA!
CROSTOSA!
OOH, YOU BOY-MAD BIKE!
AT LEAST I'M NOT A MANSHY ZITELLA!
I'M NOT, YOU LITTLE BITCH!
PUZZOLENTE!
FEDERA!
LIMONE!
TOZZA!
LUCERTOLA!
MELMOSA!
BIRILLA!
SLITTA!!
OH! THERE'S THE PIPS - I'M OUT OF CHANGE.
DOOP DOOP DOOP DOOP DOOP
QUICK-BEFORE YOU GO-
YOU'LL BE FINISHED WITH MY TINY TV?
sigh - YESSS.
SO I CAN HAVE IT BACK?
OK.- I'LL SEND IT DOWN.
TA-MISS YOU, SIS.
-DON'T GET SQUASHED OR MASHED!
-AND YOU-CIAO, SIS.
(prrrrrr
AH WELL.
♪... THERE WERE NEVER SUCH DEVOTED SISTERS!

7.51: "Jawney inter Space"

Internal...

OH, HERE YOU ALL ARE...
C'EST MAGNIFIQUE, MAIS CE N'EST PAS LA BOULE

ALL RIGHT THEN EVERYBODY, LISTEN UP. MY OTHER SELF IS SETTLED IN. ACTING ON MY INSTRUCTIONS - BASED ON MY MEMORY - SHE HAS ESTABLISHED HERSELF IN THE ROOM NEXT TO WHERE THE PROFESSOR OPENED THE PORTAL...

SHE'S ALSO GOT THE PHONY PAPERWORK NEEDED, COURTESY OF OUR AGENTS, INCLUDING A FAKE STUDENT'S UNION CARD, BASED ON ONE PINCHED FROM SOMEONE'S POCKET.
I DON'T THINK I APPROVE OF THEFT - NOT TO MENTION OUSTING THAT POOR GIRL FROM HER ROOM.

IT'S HARDLY THEFT - I DID HAND IT IN AS LOST WHEN IT WAS FINISHED WITH.
STILL...

LOOK - IT'S DONE AND IT WAS NECESSARY - O.K.?
- I DON'T WANT TO HAVE TO PULL THE "I'M THE LEADER AROUND HERE" ROUTINE!
...ZERE IS NO NEED TO BE ZO TETCHY, MAM'SELLE.

SORRY... I'VE HAD A PRETTY STRESSFUL SIX MONTHS. IT'S BEEN KIND OF FUN, BUT I'VE HAD TO BE ON MY GUARD ALL THE TIME...

...WHICH BRINGS ME TO THE MAIN THING I WANT TO TALK ABOUT - I'M GOING TO TAKE A BIT OF A BREAK IN COLD SLEEP FOR A WHILE TO RECUPERATE...

...SO WHILE I'M UNAVAILABLE, YOU LOT ARE IN CHARGE.
C'EST DESTIN!
OTTERLY WILL SIT IN AS REGENT...
DWENG WILL... - WHERE'S DWENG?
-He's off on a drinking binge with a bunch of rowdy old Norse sub-deities!
SLAM!
IS HE NOW? WELL, I-
FOOD GOOD LOVE DEAD
WHURRGGLE!
DWENG?
WHOOSH
HOME
GOT NOTHING IN
FOOD GOOD LOVE DEAD
SPLUMPH!
MUST EAT. GOT MUNCHIES
FOOD GOOD LOVE DEAD
SKWIJ! SQUIRK!
HUNGRY
SMAK SMAK
FOOD GOOD
TRY FRIDGE
FRIGINELLE
HAVE TO DO SOMETHING ABOUT THAT - BUILD WALL MAYBE TO KEEP BACK ICE.
FOOD GOOD
NASTY
HOT
AH!

SMELL GOOD - NEEDS BULK THOUGH
FOOD GOOD LOVE DEAD
BLOOP
WHAT CAN PUT IN?
FOOD GOOD
AHA!
GREYS
FOOD GOOD
YOU DEAD MEAT!
?
??
RRIP!
CHOP CHOP CHOP CHOP!
SPLOSH!
DONE ENOUGH! NOT WAIT NO LONGER!!
GLUP GLUP GLUP
FOOD GOOD LOVE
WHOOMF!!
AAAHHH!
?
!!!
FOOD GOOD LOVE DEAD
YERG! WORST EVER!!
MUST KEEP RECIPE!

...Combustion!

jocasta, inside a dream
...SOUNDS LIKE PANDA'S STILL GOT THAT FLU' OF HERS...
COUGH COUGH COUGH
BASTARD BASTARD EARTH GERMS!!
COUGH
OH WELL- AT LEAST I KNOW I'LL LIVE...
LAST TIME I SAW HER SHE LOOKED LIKE DEATH... ...NEVER MIND-I'LL POP ROUND WITH SOME GRAPES AND A TOILET ROLL TOMORROW...
cough cough
CLICK
... HEY JO, WHERE YOU GOING WITH THAT MONEY... ...I'M GOIN' DOWN THE CHEMIST'S TO GET SOME STREPSILS FOR PANDA... ...WOH YEAH...
...BIBBLE BABBLE BOBBLE...MOLEEDS.. ..PENTATEUCH OF THE COZMOGININNY OH THE HOOMANITY Noo Noo not the comfy chair
zzz
...IF YOU CAN JUST GET YOUR MIND TOGETHER, THEN COME ON ACROSS TO ME...
...WE'LL HOLD HANDS AND WATCH THE SUNRISE FROM THE BOTTOM OF THE SEA — — BUT FIRST — ARE YOU EXPERIENCED?...
UH... WELL, CAN'T STAY- HEY, TURN ME LOOSE, BABY- ...GOTTA GET AWAY... I GOT TO MOVE ON...
-HELL, I'M STONE FREE TO DO WHAT I PLEASE- -I'M GOIN' ON DOWN THE HIGHWAY...
BYE BYE BABY! ...
POPPLE PLOP POP...
POOP POOP!
POLLO POP!
AH... THAT'S BETTER.

SHE FLIES WHO FLIES!
whee
wheee!
WHEEEE!!
HELLO! I'M PANDA PETE - I'M SEXUALLY AMBIGUOUS AND I NEVER GROW OLD!!
GOSH!
BE WITH ME!
HERE I GO!...
JUST CALL ME LUCIFER
VOLANS
CANOPUS
G2
R10
PROMINENCE
"FOR EVERY MAN, EVERY WOMAN AND EVERY CHILD ON EARTH, THERE IS A STAR..."
CHROMOSPHERE
I LIVE IN A PIRATE SHIP
GEMINI
CORONA
PHOTOSPHERE
COR!!
THE TEMPERATURE OF EVEN THE CENTRE OF A SUNSPOT IS OVER NINE THOUSAND ONE HUNDRED DEGREES
SECOND STAR ON THE LEFT AND STRAIGHT ON TILL MORNING
LIMB DARKENING
CYGNUS
IS LEFT RIGHT?
I'M SUBLIME
WHAT'S THAT?
I HIDE IN THE THE DARK!
VIRGO
SHE'S THE TWINKLE IN MY I
CRUX
HERE'S A MANGY FLYING GLASS...
MICROSCOPIUM

"THE STARS THAT SHINE, AND THE STARS THAT SHRINK..."
"IN THE FACE OF STAGNATION, THE WATERS RUN..."
"... BEFORE YOUR EYES..."
PEEK-A-BOO!
I CAN SEE YOU!...
STOP!
I AM MAAT, GODDESS OF TRUTH AND CONSISTENCY.
YOU CANNOT GO TOO FAR.
YOU MUST BECOME JUNG AGAIN...
YOWP!
GOING DOWN!...
FALLING, FALLING, FALLING, FALLING . . .
OH DEAR - IT'S MY 11th BIRTHDAY AGAIN...
NEVER MIND...
I HAVE MY LITTLE PEACH
MY MOTHER GAVE TO ME
I KEEP IT IN MY POUCH...
...HIDDEN IN MY PEACH POUCH...
I LOVE TO STROKE ITS FUZZY SKIN
OUCH!
BUMP
AHUM-AN-AHOO
AN-AHUM-AN-AHA
AN-AHO-ANAHUM...
...CAN YOU SEE WHAT IT IS YET ?

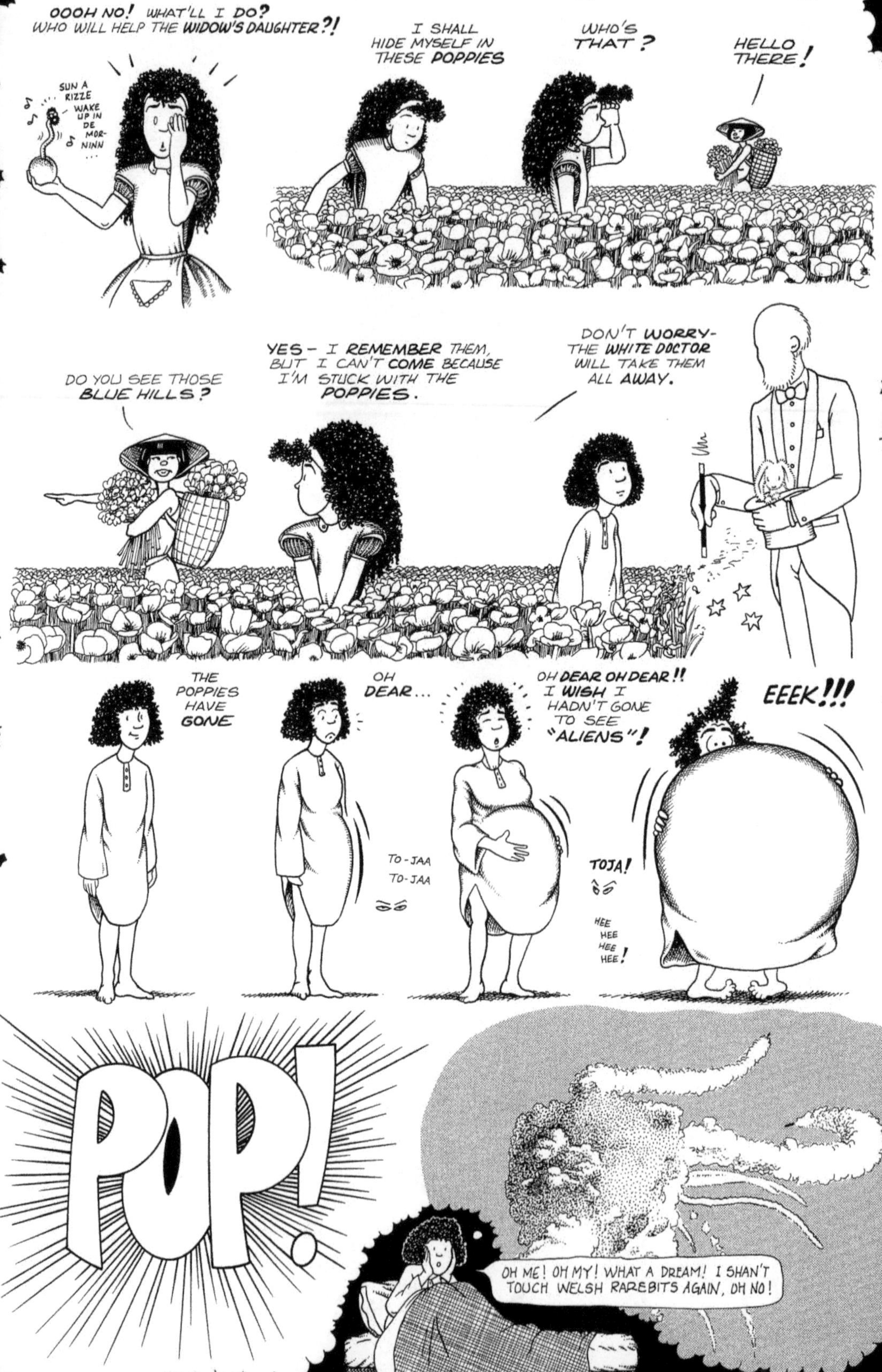
OOOH NO! WHAT'LL I DO?
WHO WILL HELP THE WIDOW'S DAUGHTER?!
SUN A RIZZE WAKE UP IN DE MOR-NINN...
I SHALL HIDE MYSELF IN THESE POPPIES
WHO'S THAT?
HELLO THERE!
DO YOU SEE THOSE BLUE HILLS?
YES - I REMEMBER THEM, BUT I CAN'T COME BECAUSE I'M STUCK WITH THE POPPIES.
DON'T WORRY- THE WHITE DOCTOR WILL TAKE THEM ALL AWAY.
THE POPPIES HAVE GONE
OH DEAR...
TO-JAA
TO-JAA
OH DEAR OH DEAR!! I WISH I HADN'T GONE TO SEE "ALIENS"!
TOJA!
HEE HEE HEE HEE!
EEEK!!!
POP!
OH ME! OH MY! WHAT A DREAM! I SHAN'T TOUCH WELSH RAREBITS AGAIN, OH NO!

Interlude: Metamorphosis

CHUG CHUG CHUG

PHARP! PHRAPP!

① REMAIN UPRIGHT ② BRUSH TEETH ③ MOUTHWASH ④ BLOW NOSE

⑤ CHECK ROOTS ⑥ WASH & RINSE ⑦ DO ROOTS & RINSE ⑧ WASH FACE

GLUP

⑨ DRY HAIR ⑩ DO EYEBROWS ⑪ CONTACTS IN ⑫ "BIO-TAN" PILLS

THIRTY-TWO...
THIRTY-THREE...

⑬ MOISTURISER ⑭ MASCARA ⑮ BRUSH HAIR ⑯ ECCE FEMINA!

3 Birthdays

November 8th '86 (#1): Petra's Letter

HAPPY TWENTIETH, DEAR.
AAAGH!
-DON'T SAY 20!
URRGH... I'M GETTING OLD...
...HERE YOU ARE!
OO!
OO!
OO!
OO!
... A BOTTLE OF SHAMPOO-
-"FOR GREASY HAIR!"
-UH HUH!...
ZOG
GREASY
-WHAT?-
"CRIME AND PUNISHMENT"-
-IN ITALIAN!!
COSMIC! THIS'LL TAKE ME MONTHS TO READ-
-THANKS!!!
DELITTO e CASTIGO
DOSTOIEVSKI
EDIZIONE FINTA
-groan-
OHH RIIIGGHT...
... A LITTLE BLACK ADDRESS BOOK!
SUBTLE-SKI MOMSKI!
DID YOU GET A CARD FROM JO?
YES-HERE IT IS. THERE'S AN ALBUM TOKEN-THAT CAN GO TOWARD MY SET OF 'DAS RHEINGOLD'- -AND A LETTER.
HIPPY YARD BATH
WELL? WHAT DOES IT SAY?
HANG ON! JUST A MO...

Hallo Mama and Pet'
Hope everyone is well back home and that the Watchman T.V. got back in one piece! Nothing much interesting has happened to me personally (as usual!), but I have made a strange new friend called Panda (really Sandra, but sometimes she wears enough eye makeup to look like one!!!) She's a first year student ~~in~~ from Thailand who stays in the room next to me. She's really weird – throws money around like confetti, dresses in a different style practically every day, never seems to go to lectures – but she doesn't seem to have the slightest idea how anything in England works.
Here's what happened at Halloween...

... OH??

WELL, WE ONCE HAD THIS GUEST AT OUR HOUSE WHO WAS SOMEWHAT UNNERVING...

ALTHOUGH HE WAS QUITE... ... PLEASANT. HE INSISTED ON BRINGING SOME OF HIS PETS WITH HIM... WE HAD TO KEEP THEM IN THE ATTIC...

...THEY NEVER ACTUALLY HARMED US, BUT I LOST AN AWFUL LOT OF SLEEP LYING IN BED LISTENING TO THE... ... PETS... EATING THE VERMIN THAT LIVE UP THERE...

... well, anyway, she was really bugging me at the council firework display yesterday ...

... only found it on Tuesday behind the bed, and it was all covered in fluff! Urrggh!
Anyway, Happy Birthday Petra, hugs and kisses to everybody, (strokes for Winston),

la tua sorella, Jocasta

High Society

SOME TIME LATER
STUDENTS UNION
VOTE ×
Lorelei Jacobs
TODAYS MEETINGS
NOV. 12
QUESTLANDS ROOM 101
TALL WOMEN WAINWRIGHT BAR
DRAMA WAINWRIGHT FUNCTION ROOM
BONDAGE DARRAS HALL
UNIVERSITY
...THE FUNCTION ROOM'S THROUGH HERE, I THINK... ...JUST A MINUTE...
ARTH-SCARTHEN
DARTH DALE
KENDAL MINT CAKE
...I KNOW WHO THEY ARE!
ER, EXCUSE ME...
OH, HELLO.
...I WAS WONDERING HOW TALL I HAVE TO BE TO JOIN THE TALL WOMEN'S SOCIETY.
JOHNSON TOR
WELL, OUR CONSTITUTION SAYS 5'9", BUT WE'D PASS 5'8" IF YOU RECKONED YOU WERE STILL GROWING.
XMAS PARTY
OH DEAR- I STOPPED AT 5'7" A LONG TIME AGO.
NEVER MIND.
- DID YOU HAVE SOME SORT OF HEIGHTISM PROBLEM YOU WERE WORRIED ABOUT?
ER, NO, I WAS MAINLY WONDERING ABOUT SHOES. - I TAKE AN 8½ AND A LOT OF THEM STOP AT 8.
LET ME GUESS- YOU EITHER GET EIGHTS THAT PINCH OR TRY TO FIND NINES IN MEN'S STYLES-
RIGHT?
RIGHT.
TRY THEM- "CHALUPAS" - WE GET ALL OURS THERE, 'COS THEY GO UP TO ELEVEN.
THANKS, AND, ERR... ...BY THE WAY, WHO'S THAT SITTING OVER THERE?
OH, HER - THAT'S ELAINE. SHE'S A BREAKAWAY FACTION. - CALLS HERSELF THE "TALL VOODOO FETISH WOMAN" SOCIETY...

HUM... STRANGE!
OH WELL - NICE MEETING YOU - -THANKS FOR THE CARD!
FUNCTION RO
GLAD TO BE OF HELP.
WELL, THIS IS THE RIGHT ROOM - - I WONDER WHO'S IN CHARGE?
HULLO -
HEY, YOU!..
HAMLET
-YOU'RE JO WHATSIT FROM NEXT DOOR IN ETHEL MERMAN HALL, AREN'T YOU?
..METHINKS T'IS LIKE A WEASEL..
THERE'S A DAISY...
OH YES - YOU'RE KIM 'ANTHROPOLOGY' OR SOMETHING (?)
ANTHROPOPHAGOS - THAT'S RIGHT. WHAT ARE YOU DOING HERE?
- I SUPPOSE I COULD ASK THE SAME THING...
- I MEAN I JUST CAME HERE ABOUT JOINING...
NOR DO NOT SAW THE AIR TOO MUCH WITH YOUR HAND..
HE SAID I WAS A FISHMONGER - HE IS FAR GONE...
OH, AH'M HERE DOING THE COSTUME DESIGNS. -IT'LL BE LIZ YOU'LL BE WANTING TO SEE - CAN'T MISS HER, SHE'S THE ONE WI' THE BIG HEID...
... I MEAN, SHOULD WE BE AFRAID TO CHALLENGE THE OPPRESSED IMAGE THAT OPHELIA REPRESENTS...
ER, EXCUSE ME...
- JUST A SECOND, LOVE - ... DO WE PLAY IT DOWN TO PRESENT A POSITIVE ROLE IMAGE, OR DO WE PARODY AND THEREBY SUBVERT?
...I'D LIKE TO JOIN, PLEASE.
OH, PARDON ME A SEC WOULD YOU, RUSS - - I'M SORRY, DARLING, I THOUGHT YOU WERE SOMEBODY ELSE - - CAN I HELP?
I... WOULD LIKE... TO JOIN... THE DRAMA SOCIETY.
PLEASE
OH, SPLENDID! WE CAN ALWAYS USE NEW BLOOD, NEW TALENT, NEW IDEAS, MORE INPUT FOR DEBATE, THAT SORT OF THING. - TELL ME, DEAR, WOULD YOU BE INTERESTED IN HELPING OUT, SCENERY, COSTUMES, PROMPTS AND SO FORTH, OR IS STRUTTING THE BOARDS MORE YOUR CUP OF TEA, HMMM ??
- WHEW! -
WELL... I HAVE ACTED BEFORE -
- I WAS IN A PRODUCTION AT HIGH SCHOOL, CALLED...

...Three Sisters (Who Are Not Sisters)
by Gertrude Stein
(massively abridged)
WE ARE 3 SISTERS, WHO ARE NOT SISTERS. WE ARE ORPHANS.
WE ARE 2 BROTHERS WHO ARE BROTHERS. WE ARE NOT ORPHANS, NOT AT ALL; (WE ARE NOT EVEN TALL.)
...AND NOW THAT EVERYONE KNOWS JUST WHAT WE ARE, WHAT ARE WE GOING TO DO?
I HAVE AN IDEA, A FINE IDEA. LET US PLAY A PLAY. LET IT BE A MURDER.
OH YES!
LET'S BEGIN.
LOOK AT THE CHAIR. - WHICH CHAIR? THE ONLY CHAIR. - I CAN'T SEE THE ONLY CHAIR!
...THERE IS NO CHAIR THERE. - WHICH ONE IS GOING TO MURDER WHICH ONE?
WAIT AND SEE
OH! HE'S DEAD - SYLVESTER IS DEAD - SOMEBODY MURDERED HIM... SAMUEL KILLED HIM! AND WHERE IS HELEN?...
THERE IS HELEN - - AND SHE'S DEAD!! OH!!!
AH HAH! I AM A POLICEMAN, BUT I KILLED BOTH OF THEM, AND NOW I AM GOING TO DO SOME MORE KILLING
(HEH HEH HEH!)
...I AM LOOKING FOR HELEN.
AH HAH! YOU KILLED HER - NOW I AM GOING TO DO SOME KILLING
OOH! NOT ME, DEAR, KIND POLICEMAN...
OH NO! ANOTHER ONE! NOW I AM THE ONLY ONE!...
I AM SYLVESTER, AND I'M DEAD. EVERYONE THINKS IT WAS SAMUEL WHO KILLED ME BUT IT WAS SHE
I AM HELEN AND I AM DEAD; AND EVERYONE THINKS IT WAS SAMUEL WHO KILLED ME - NOT AT ALL, IT WAS SHE
I AM ELLEN, AND I AM DEAD (OH SO DEAD) - IT WAS SHE (OH YES) IT WAS SHE
IT WAS NOT SAMUEL WHO KILLED THEM, IT WAS SHE. AND WHO CAN SHE BE? CAN SHE BE ME? IT CAN NOT BE! ...BUT PERHAPS IT IS. WELL, IF IT IS THEN I WILL KILL SAMUEL AND THEN THEY WILL ALL BE DEAD.
THEY SAY I DID NOT KILL THEM THEY SAY IT WAS SHE! I WILL FIND HER - I WILL KILL HER!
OH! IT IS SO! SHE IS THE ONE. SHE HAS KILLED ALL OF THEM. SHE HAS ALL THE GLORY...
I KILLED HIM, YES I DID, AND NOW THEY ARE ALL DEAD. WELL, THERE IS NO USE LIVING ALONE, SO I WILL KILL MYSELF...
AH - THAT IS POISON...
GLUP!
SATIRE
WE ARE DEAD
WE ARE DEAD
SHE KILLED US
WE ARE DEAD
LALALA LAAA
LA LA LA LAAA
...DID WE ACT IT? ARE WE DEAD? DO WE FEEL... FUNNY?
OF COURSE WE ARE NOT DEAD
...I AM NOT DEAD - I AM AN ORPHAN AND A SISTER WHO IS NOT A SISTER, BUT I AM NOT DEAD.
IT IS VERY NICE INDEED NOT TO BE DEAD.
OH SHUT UP, EVERYBODY - IT IS TIME TO GO TO BED, ORPHANS AND ALL, AND BROTHERS TOO.
CLAP.
CLAP.
CLAP.
- I KNEW WE SHOULD'VE DONE "LOOK AND LONG"...

November 22nd '86 (#2): Panda's Pizza

IT'S CERTAINLY ... DIFFERENT.
OH, IT'S JUST A FEW THINGS I PICKED UP TO REMIND ME OF HOME. -I'D PREFER A BIGGER ROOM, OF COURSE.
- whew -
WELL ANYHOW -
I JUST POPPED ROUND TO SEE IF YOU WERE DOING ANYTHING. SATURDAYS TEND TO LEAVE ME AT A LOOSE END - I'M REDUCED TO READING THIS NEWSPAPER.
ANYTHING INTERESTING IN IT?
Today
Reagan: I knew nothing about Iran
LET'S SEE... ... I HAVEN'T READ THE HOROSCOPE YET... ... HERE IT IS:
"VIRGO: AN UNEXPECTED GIFT MAY BRING YOU MUCH LASTING HAPPINESS. TODAY IS A GOOD DAY TO DEAL WITH LONG-STANDING PROBLEMS WHICH HAVE BEEN NIGGLING YOU, AND YOU MAY RECEIVE HELP FROM A MEMBER OF THE OPPOSITE SEX. A VISIT FROM RELATIVES IS LIKELY"...
HUMM - SO MUCH FOR THAT. WHEN'S YOUR BIRTHDAY?
ERRR... WE RECKON DATES DIFFERENTLY WHERE I COME FROM - BUT I DO KNOW I WAS BORN ON THE CUSP OF SCORPIO AND SAGITTARIUS.
SCORPIO AND SAGITTARIUS...
BLIMEY! THAT'S TODAY!!
OOH! IT'S MY BIRTHDAY?! -AND I NEVER KNEW!!
nothing about Iran
-SO HOW MANY DOES THAT MAKE - IF YOU DON'T MIND ME ASKING?
UH OH - HOW OLD AM I SUPPOSED TO BE?...
N-N-NINETEEN (?)
-A MERE GIRL! PHOO - YOU MAKE ME FEEL OLD!
NEVER MIND - WHAT DO PEOPLE DO ON THEIR BIRTHDAY ROUND HERE?
GOSH - WELL, I'D HAVE GOT YOU A PRESENT IF I'D HAD HAD A BIT MORE WARNING. -I COULD TAKE YOU OUT FOR A MEAL OR SOMETHING...
PIZZA PIZZA PIZZA!
PTU! SHE'S HERE WITH HER PIZZAS AGAIN!
BOING BOING
I'VE NEVER SEEN ANYBODY FALL FOR ITALIAN DISHES SO FAST!
VERY WELL - LET'S DO THAT. I'LL GO GET MY HAT AND MEET YOU BY THE LOBBY WHEN YOU'RE READY.
MMM! -O.K.

LATER
♪... ZUM ZUM ZUM... ...WONDER WHAT SHE'LL BE WEARING TODAY... ♪
...HMM, WHAT'S THIS? ...NEW PINBALL MACHINE - "CUBAN MISSILE CRISIS?"
We only use 10% of our mental potential
TO HAND OUT THESE FLYERS
DRAMA SOC PRESENT HAMLET 7:15 DEC 9th
"SCORE BY STRIKING MISSILE BUMPERS AND USING ABM FLIPPERS. HIT 'FRIGATE CONFRONTATION' TARGET TO ADVANCE DEFCON INDICATOR. EXTRA BONUS BALL AWARDED FOR LIGHTING K-E-N-N-E-D-Y OR K-R-U-S-C-H-E-V IN SEQUENCE. 'BAY OF PIGS' TRAP DEDUCTS 2 BALLS. LIGHT CASTRO ROLL-OVER AT DEFCON 3 TO ACTIVATE EXTRA PLAY FEATURE IN ILLUMINATED ICBM SILO ZONE... HITTING 'HIT' TARGET WILL CAUSE 'LITE' LIGHT TO LIGHT..."
"...LIGHTING RASH DIPLOMACY TARGET WHILST AT DEFCON 1 WILL INITIATE TACTICAL NUCLEAR PLAY WITH 1 BALL PER MEGATON AS SHOWN ON STOCKPILE READING. POSSIBLE BONUS IS 200,000,000 POINTS MINUS MEGADEATHS INCURRED DURING 4½ MINUTES"
...DUBIOUS TASTE PINBALL? WHATEVER NEXT?...
COO-EE!
HELLO! WHAT D'YOU THINK?
URK!
WHAT ON EARTH ARE YOU WEARING?!
IT'S MADE OUT OF HARP SEALS-
-MINK'S TOO EXPENSIVE EVEN FOR ME!
YOU CAN'T WEAR THAT!!
OF COURSE I CAN-
IT'S BOUND TO SNOW - IT'S BEEN UNBELIEVABLY COLD LATELY.
YEAH - ABOUT FIFTY FAHRENHEIT! -OH, COME ON, PANDA- -DON'T WEAR FUR!
...DON'T DO IT!
POUT!
"...FUR'S FOR FOOLS!"
IT'S TOO COLD!
sigh ALL RIGHT, ALL RIGHT- DO WHAT YOU LIKE-
-BUT IF YOU GET BLOWN UP BY ANIMAL LIBERATIONISTS, DON'T COME RUNNING TO ME!..
HMM HMMM HMM HMMM

I'M LOOKING FORWARD TO THIS- - WE SHOULD GO AND DO IT ON YOUR BIRTHDAY TOO! WHEN IS IT- SEEING AS YOU KNOW MINE NOW?
YOU'RE OUT OF LUCK, I'M AFRAID. MINE'S SEPTEMBER- -BEFORE TERM STARTS
KICK
OH DEAR- THERE MUST BE SOME OTHER TIME- I WANT TO GIVE YOU A PRESENT. DO PEOPLE CELEBRATE HALF BIRTHDAYS HERE?
I DON'T THINK SO! THERE'S ALWAYS CHRISTMAS, OF COURSE.
...WHICH IS WHEN?
NO... NO... ...DON'T SHOUT AT HER! -SHE'S PROBABLY A BUDDHIST OR SOMETHING!!!
DECEMBER...TWENTY-FIFTH. WE BREAK UP FOR IT, DON'T WE? HENCE THE NAME: "CHRISTMAS VACATION!"
OH YESSS, OF COURSE (!?) HOW SILLY OF ME -I'LL GET YOU A CHRISTMAS PRESENT, THEN...
EEEK!!!
- I CAN'T AFFORD MANY MORE SLIP-UPS LIKE THAT- -IT'S DOUBLE HOMEWORK ON PEAR'S CYCLOPAEDIA FOR ME!
... YOU CAN BE SO WEIRD SOMETIMES.
...LIKE SOME BOGUS FOOL WHO'S OBVIOUSLY NOT FROM THAILAND MAYBE? -SHIT!!!
WEIRD?
...IN WHAT WAY WEIRD??
...FORGETTING WHAT DATE CHRISTMAS IS. WEARING A DIFFERENT OUTFIT EVERY SINGLE DAY...
-DON'T BE SO PAROCHIAL! WE DON'T DO CHRISTMAS WHERE I COME FROM.
AS FOR THE OUTFITS, WELL- -WHEN I SEE THE RANGE OF THINGS PEOPLE WEAR OVER HERE, I WANT TO TRY THEM ALL OUT!!
HMM. BETTER NOT GO TOO MAD, OR YOU'LL RUN OUT OF MONEY!
YES, MOTHER!
PHEW!
HI, JO!

OH HI, STEVE – I DON'T THINK YOU'VE MET HAVE YOU – THIS IS SANDRA –
SANDRA – STEVE
HELLO! – STEVE BRONTOSAURUS. SPELT BRONTOSAURUS BUT PRONOUNCED 'BONSER' – GOD KNOWS WHY!...
HELLO
SO – WHERE ARE Y' OFF TO?
WE'RE GOING TO THE "HUTLAND Co" FOR A PIZZA – IT'S SANDRA'S BIRTHDAY.
IT IS
OH – CONGRATULATIONS! HERE – TELL YOU WHAT, YOU CAN HAVE SOME INVITES FOR OUR XMAS PARTY!
A PARTY!?
THAT SOUNDS INTERESTING! WE MUST GO, JO!
HMM...
HMMMMM... ...THING IS... ...WELL... ...ERMMMM...
ERM... HMMMM? HMMMM...
HEY SANDRA – YOU PERSUADE HER FOR ME, WOULD YOU? I'VE GOT TO GET BACK TO 'RACKY ROAD.
OKAY.
PLEEASE CAN WE GO TO THE PARTY?? – YOU KNOW ME – I WOULD PROBABLY MAKE A COMPLETE FOOL OF MYSELF IF YOU DIDN'T COME AND KEEP ME CORRECT!
– ALL RIGHT! I'LL GO – JUST LAY OFF THE JUMPER! ...
LET'S MOVE ON A LITTLE – PAUSING FOR SOME HIGHLIGHTS OF THE PIZZA ORGY!
MMMM!
Hut Land
Birthday Girl Souvenir
THAT'S A 'SMALL'?
Hut Land
Birthday Girl Souvenir
Hut Hat
Hut Land
Birthday Girl Souvenir

Interlude : Walk the Dog

Roar of the Greasepaint...

...I think it be no other, but e'en so:
...WE USED TO PUT ON SOME REALLY SPLENDID MASQUES BACK HOME ...I THINK THAT'S THE WORD...
... A little ere the mightiest Julius fell,
...I USED TO WEAR MY DAD'S HAT AND PRETEND TO BE THE, ER... KING OF SIAM...
The graves stood tenantless, and the sheeted dead Did squeak and gibber in the Roman streets:
GIGGLE!
OH NO! I DAREN'T GO ON NOW!
LOOK- JUST RELAX- THINK ABOUT SOMETHING ELSE...
COME HERE...
RIGHT- YOU'LL LIKE THIS - HERE'S SOME QUOTES FROM "MACBETH"...
AAARGH!
-YOU CAN'T SAY THAT- IT'S BAD LUCK!
WHAT- "MACBETH?"
YOU SAID IT AGAIN!
URGHH- -NOW I'M BOUND TO MESS UP...
...Where we shall find him most conveniently.
WHOOPS! THAT'S IT- " ENTER KING, QUEEN, HAMLET, (BLAH BLAH BLAH), LORDS AND ATTENDANTS - THAT'S YOU!
AWW... I DON'T WANNA!
JUST GET OUT THERE AND ATTEND! -GOOD LUCK!!
YOU AREN'T SUPPOSED TO SAY THAT EITHER!...
TRIP- THUD!
OH DEAR- -YOU HAVEN'T BROKEN ANYTHING, HAVE YOU?

December 19th '86 (#3): Steve's Party

RIVERSID
I CAN HARDLY BELIEVE IT- -I'VE JUST BEEN TO A SHOW FEATURING A MAN IN A FALSE HEAD ARGUING WITH A CARD- -BOARD PUPPET AND SINGING NASALLY ABOUT FOOTBALL...
frank idebottom
marionation ur dec '86 5–19th 00 pm

...AND I ACTUALLY LIKED IT!
"OOOH, FOOTBALL IS REELY FANGTASTEEC!"
-AND YOU CALLED ME WEIRD!

IT WAS FUN, THOUGH, WASN'T IT?
YES – BUT THE NIGHT IS STILL YOUNG! - - WE STILL HAVE THAT PARTY TO GO TO YET!

ohh SUGAR- I HAD HOPED SHE'D FORGOTTEN ABOUT THAT...
HMM...
YESSS...
WELL, IF YOU'RE STILL UP TO IT, OF COURSE ...

-I CERTAINLY AM! POINT ME IN THE RIGHT DIRECTION!
sigh IT'S THIS WAY...
TAPITY! TAPITY!

MMMM...
...I LOVE LOOKING AT THE MOON. IT JUST HANGS THERE IN THE SKY LIKE A BIG ROUND BALL... AS IF IT WAS CLOSE ENOUGH TO TOUCH.
HMM.

DUMP DUMP DUM
...THIS IS THE PLACE.
KNOCK KNOCK

BOM BOM BO
OH, HULLO- -HERE FOR THE PARTY?
JUST TRY AND STOP US!

HERE'S MY INVITATION
AH- I DON'T THINK I'VE GOT MINE!

BOM BOM
THAT'S O.K.-
-SHE'S WITH ME!...
BOM
OH, HALLO!
HI, JO.
HI, STEVE! HI, JACKIE!
IT'S SANDRA PANDA, ISN'T IT? I SEE YOU DRAGGED JO ALONG — THAT MUST'VE TAKEN SOME DOING!!
WELL, I NEEDED SOMEBODY TO SHOW ME WHERE THE PARTY WAS, DIDN'T I?
HAR HAR!
=COUGH=
D'YOU KNOW ANYONE HERE AT ALL?
APART FROM YOU AND JO, NOT REALLY.
WELL, ER...
COUGH!
LOOK, ER, SORRY TO LEAVE YOU, BUT I THINK I'M NEEDED TO TRY AND GET MARNIE OUT OF THE BATH-ROOM OR SOMETHING!?..
OH! FAIR ENOUGH.
THIS IS A FUNNY PARTY -IT'S SO CROWDED.
THEY USUALLY ARE. STUDENT FLATS AREN'T EXACTLY BUILT FOR BALLROOM DANCING!
WHAT ARE YOU UP TO?
EH?
NO DANCING?
SOMETIMES -IF THEY CAN CLEAR A SPACE BIG ENOUGH.
RAT TAT TAT
?
-I SAW YOU, DROOLING OVER THAT GIRL THAT JUST CAME IN.
I WASN'T! I BARELY KNOW HER!
HMM... I'M THIRSTY. ARE THESE DRINKS FOR EVERYBODY?
SORT OF- -WE REALLY SHOULD HAVE BROUGHT A BOTTLE.
HUH! YOU'RE PATHETIC WHEN YOU TRY TO LIE!...
BUT-
I HOPE THEY HAVE SOME PERRIER TOO.
ORANG JUICE
CIDER
PERRIER WATER? YOU'LL BE LUCKY- WE'RE STUCK WITH DRAUGHT "STUDENT PERRIER" FROM THE TAP!
JUST KEEP AWAY FROM HER IF YOU KNOW WHAT'S GOOD FOR YOU!
I SWEAR BY MY SISTER'S LIFE I WON'T LAY A FINGER ON HER.
OH NO - I MUST HAVE PERRIER- MY er ELDER RELATIVE TOLD ME NOT TO DRINK THE WATER OVER HERE.

HMM - THERE'S SOME ORANGE JUICE HERE...
HI, NADIA!
DEBBIE?
?
ORANG JUICE
OH! PERHAPS NOT...
WHAT DO YOU MEAN IT ISN'T FANCY DWESS?
ORANG JUICE
HI, JO. - SORRY I HAD TO GO OFF JUST NOW -
HOW ARE YOU?..
I'VE NOTHING ELSE TO WEAR!
OH, ALL RIGHT...
COURSEWORK'S GETTING A BIT-
-'COS I'M FURIOUS AT THAT BLOODY STEVE. HE'S SO OBVIOUS! YOU MUST HAVE SEEN HIM OGGLING YOUR FRIEND THERE...
- OH! DEBBIE! MIND OUT FOR THAT POOL OF-
WAS HE? I NEVER—
SQUISH!
... I CAN'T UNDERSTAND HOW HE CAN LIVE WITH HIMSELF - - I BET HE EVEN CHASES AFTER THAT NADIA FROM UPSTAIRS...
HUH! MEN, EH? YOU-
URGHH!...
... WELL, NEVER MIND MY PROBLEMS, YOU JUST HAVE FUN, EH? - WATCH OUT FOR STEVE, THOUGH - HE'LL PROBABLY BE AFTER YOU NEXT!..
EURYTHMICS
AAARGH!! TOO MUCH PARANOIA!..
OH GWEAT- NOW I'VE WUINED THE WABBIT SUIT...
... BELIEVE THAT GOLF IS A FASCIST TOOL OF THE BOURGEOISIE, TAKING UP ABOUT A SQUARE KILOMETRE OF WHAT COULD BE DECENT COMMON LAND TO PLAY OUT POWER FANTASY STRUGGLES AMONG MIDDLE MANAGEMENT...
UMM
... SO WHAT WE IN THE 'PSYCHO GOLF' MOVEMENT DO IS TO INFILTRATE AND SUBVERT GOLF CLUBS BY JOINING THEM, AND TURNING UP FOR THE FIRST GAME IN BONDAGE GEAR AND MOHAWKS - BUT WEARING THE RIGHT SHOES OF COURSE...
ER...
I THINK I'D LIKE TO SEE THAT - I'VE GOT A REPUTATION FOR WEARING STRANGE CLOTHES MYSELF.
I CAN SEE THAT! DO YOUR FOLKS HASSLE YOU TO DRESS NORMALLY? I KNOW MINE DO.
NO, NOT ANY MORE - I PRETTY MUCH HAVE THE WHOLE HOUSE TO MYSELF BACK HOME, AND I DO WHAT I LIKE.
WHERE'S THAT?
OH, IT'S A BIG SPRAWLING THING IN THAILAND,...

oh POOP – I DON'T SEE WHY I SHOULD HANG AROUND HER ALL NIGHT – – WHAT ARE WE, ENGAGED?...
HA HA HA
HMMM... MUSTN'T GO NEAR STEVE, OR JACKIE'LL THINK WE'RE AN ITEM... CAN'T SEE MIKE OR JOANNA ANYWHERE...
HEY, YOU TWO – WATCH OUT FOR THAT POOL OF – OH.
MMM MMM
...WHO'S IN HERE?...
(OH BOY – JONA LEWIE COUNTRY ALREADY!..)
KITCHEN TID ROTA
STEVE MON
Nadia TUES
STEVE WED
Judy THU
PAUL FRID
Nadia SAT
PAUL SUN
STAR TREK
FREE CORNFLAKE
JUDYS SUGAR
OH – THERE'S ROSIE SIMONS...
EGGZ EGGZ EGGZ
SIZZLE! CRACKLE!
ROSIE! WHAT BRINGS YOU HERE?
Hullo! ...Basically, we're trying to put together another issue of "Bog" – we're the Women Cartoonist Society, by the way...
POACHED BOILED OR FRIED...
WOW! I DIDN'T KNOW YOU WERE IN THAT.
Oh yeah.
Let me introduce you...
SALUT
HI
H'LO
Judy de Sade...
Carole Day...
Kimberley Harper.
SO 'BOG' IS YOUR MAGAZINE? IS IT ANYTHING LIKE 'VIZ'??
NO – IT ISN'T LIKE VIZ! EVERY TIME WE MENTION WE DO A COMIC, ZE PEOPLE SAY "IS IT LIKE VIZ" – IT GET VERY IRRITATEEN!
THEY'RE GOOD FOR YOUR...
Look, never mind – d'you fancy helping us bash out some ideas, 'cos we're totally blocked at the minute... ...we've got our own jug of punch too...
THHPPPP! (OH SHUT UP...)
OKAY! WHAT HAVE YOU GOT SO FAR?...
TIK TOK TIK TOK TIK TOK TIK TOK TIK TOK
WHIZZ
! ? ! * !?

MANY GLASSES LATER
SEE THIS? MY FRED GAVE ME THIS FOR EXMUS...
HEY YOU... THIMBLEY YOU'RE PHOGOGENIC –LESS TAKE YOUR PITCHER...
OH, THIS IS HOPELESS.
AND 'E WENT AND 'E WENT AND 'E WENT ...
!
FLASH
περφερτ!
HEY JO – COME QUICK – SANDRA'S IN TROUBLE!!
CLICK WHIZZ
OH BOTHERATION...
WADDYA THINK YER DOIN' WI MA BOYFRIEND? MA BOYFRIEND?!
!!!
ohh NOOOOOOO!...
SAY THAT IN ENGLISH, YA COW!!!!
OOOOH.... GO STICK YOUR HEAD UP A DEAD BEAR'S ARSE!!!
AAARGH!
SPLAT!
ALL RIGHT THAT'S ENOUGH! WE'RE GOING!...
GRR!
THRASH
KICK
OH PANDA! ARE YOU ALL RIGHT?
NNNGH!
OOH! SHE HID ME! NOBODY'S EBBER HID ME BEFORE!
LOOK LESS JUSS LEAVE BY THE BACK WAY B'FORE YOU GET INTO ENNY MORE FIGHTS!...
–IT WASN'T LIKE SHE MEANT ANYTHING TO ME, FOR GOD'S SAKE!!...

– MEANT ANYTHING?! PUT ME DOWN, YA BIG KEECH! –I'LL GIVE YE 'MEANT'!
– 'FA CATCH YOU LIKE THAT AGAIN, I'LL HA' YER NUTS FOR A NECKLACE!!!...
The bastud... ...diddet mead eddythig to hib... ...oh dear... ...waaaaaa...
WHOOOOPS... MIND OUT, IT'S ICEY...
- huck - - huck - uh-haww...
she hid me! id hurds. ...losd my stick as well...
OH, DON'T CRY... THERE THERE...
SNORK!
OHH... LESS FORGET ALL THE NASTY STUFF... ...DO SOMETHING JOLLY TO TAKE YOUR MIND OFF OF IT AN' CHEER YOU UP. ...WE'LL DO SOME CAROL SINGING...ING!
sniff
KNOCK KNOCK
HUMM... - CAN'T REMEMBER ENNY EXMUSS CAROLS...
I... WAS... BO-ORRN... UNDR'A WANNN-DRIN'... STARRR!..
snurf
SLAM!
OH WELL.
JO... ...WOULD YOU MIDE IF WE JUSD WEND HOBE?
... I THIG I'BE MISJUDGED THE MATIG RITUALS ROUD HERE... WHAD A FOOL...
NEVER FEAR – YOU STICK WITH YER AUNTY JO, AN' SHE'LL LOOK AFTER YOU, YOU'LL SEE...
EVERYTHING'S GOING TO BE ALLL...
!?
WHOOPS!
THUMP
= AAAAAAAAAAA <
JO! YOU SLIPPED! ARE YOU ALL RIGHT?
-Loooop!-
- CUUURRVE!-
- LUSSSSH!-
- gasp -
phone for HELP!
OH DEAR OH DEAR OH DEAR OH DEAR OH DEAR OH DEAR OH DEAR OH DEAR....
BLURRR!
CUUUUUD!
GWAAARR?

...LUCKY THEY PUT EMERGENCY INSTRUCTIONS IN THESE THINGS...
WHICH SERVICE PLEASE?
HELP! MY FRIEND'S FALLEN OVER AND HURT HERSELF!
...THAT'LL BE AMBULANCE THEN...
SOME TIME LATER...
...I MUST ADMIT, I'VE NEVER SEEN ANYONE BREAK BOTH TIBIAS IN A SIMPLE FALL BEFORE. I CAN ONLY ASSUME SHE WEAKENED ONE OF THEM IN A PREVIOUS KNOCK.
okee fenokee
-BUT WILL SHE BE WELL AGAIN?
...OH YES, NO DOUBT ABOUT THAT. LUCKILY THEY'RE BOTH CLEAN BREAKS. WE'LL HAVE TO KEEP HER IN FOR AT LEAST THREE WEEKS, THOUGH, AND WE'D RATHER SHE DIDN'T TRY WALKING TILL THEY'RE HEALED.
OOP
ACK
THPPP
OH- SHE CAN'T GO HOBE FOR CHRISTMAS THEN?
I WOULDN'T RECOMMEND IT...
Accident & E
RIGHT- THAT'S IT. SOON AS I'VE PHONED JO'S MOTHER, I'M OUT OF HERE. I CAN'T POSSIBLY GO BACK TO HALLS NOW WITH KIM THE PSYCHOPATH LIVING TWO DOORS AWAY...
KEEP CLEAR
...JO'S BETTER OFF WITHOUT ME ANYWAY- -NONE OF THIS WOULD HAVE HAPPENED IF I HADN'T INSISTED ON GOING TO THAT PARTY...
PROF! PROF? ARE YOU THERE?
GOOT HEAVENS, FRAULEIN- VHAT IS ZER MEANING OF ZIS?
-I CAN'T TAGE EDDY MORE - I WANT TO GO HOBE NOW. - DO WHATEVER YOU CAD.
ZIS IS MOST IRREGULAR — YOU FORGET ZAT YOU HAF ALREADY RETURNED FROM ZER FYUTURE TO OUR WORLD. VHAT YOU PROPOSE VOULD CREATE TWO PANDAS!
NASTY TIME PARADOX, HUH?
YAWOHL- MOST UNPRECEDENTED. EVEN ZIS MESSAGE IS IN DANGER OF CAUSING A PARADOX- -I CAN ONLY ADVISE YOU MUST BE SHTRONG UND TRY TO HANG ON!!
sigh
OKAY...
...SEE YOU IN APRIL THEN...
CLICK
BASTARD
BASTARD
BASTARD!
-LUCKILY KIM'S DECIDED TO MOVE IN WITH BOYFRIEND ERIC TO KEEP AN EYE ON HIM — -EH, READERS?...

Rest and Recuperation

WERE YOU REALLY?
OF COURSE...
...ANYWAY, I GOT BACK AND SAW HER STUFF HAD GONE FROM HER DOOR. I THOUGHT SHE HAD GONE HOME FOR CHRISTMAS, BUT IT TURNS OUT SHE'S MOVED IN WITH...ERIC...
?
HER BOYFRIEND? POOR PANDA - YOU REALLY FANCIED HIM DIDN'T YOU?
MMMM
SHE'S PROBABLY KEEPING AN EYE ON HIM. -NEVER MIND...
HELLO JO!
HEY LOOK-MUM! PETRA!
HOW ARE YOU DOING DEAR? WE'VE BROUGHT SOME OF THOSE "MOUNTAIN BARS" YOU LIKE, AND SOME FRUIT, OF COURSE...
OOH, TA- "SNAP!" EVEN-
-SANDRA BROUGHT SOME AS WELL. THIS IS HER, BY THE WAY!...
-OH YES! PANDA THE LOONEY!
PANDA THE WHAT?
er, PLEASED TO MEET YOU
HONESTLY-THE WAY JO GOES ON ABOUT YOU SOMETIMES, YOU'D THINK SHE FANCIED YOU!!...
NUDGE
WELL, AS YOU CAN IMAGINE, THE WHOLE FAMILY'S COMING UP FOR CHRISTMAS, SO WE CAN ONLY STAY TODAY, BUT WE'RE GOING TO BROWBEAT THE DOCTORS TO SEE HOW SOON THEY'LL LET YOU COME HOME.
HMM... I DON'T THINK I'M GOING TO MAKE XMAS SOMEHOW...
-BUT WE'LL TRY AND GET YOU OUT FOR NEW YEAR ANYWAY.
HEY! I-CAN SEE-YOUR KNI-CKERS!
PETRA! REALLY! I HAVE ENOUGH TROUBLE WITH THE WIND BLOWING UP THERE!...

12 days at Christmas / Solilique

SO, THERE WAS NOTHING TO **DO** BUT WATCH **ROTTEN CHRISTMAS T.V**, AND PLAY MY **GUITAR**. I PLAYED IT WITH **HEADPHONES** ON SO AS NOT TO DISTURB THE **OTHER** PATIENTS, BUT YOU COULD STILL HEAR THE **STRINGS** A BIT. I ASKED THE GIRL IN THE NEXT BED IF SHE **MINDED**, AND SHE SAID '**NO** - IT SOUNDS LIKE THE **RADIO** BIT OFF "**WISH YOU WERE HERE**", OR LIKE '**A THOUSAND TWANGLING INSTRUMENTS**'. IT TURNS OUT **HER** PARENTS WERE "**TEMPEST**" GROUPIES **TOO** - HER NAME WAS **ARIEL**. **SHE** GOT OUT FOR **CHRISTMAS EVE**. LUCKY **COW**.

SO I'D BE LYING THERE **STRUMMING**, USUALLY, WHEN **PANDA** CAME TO **VISIT ME**. SHE CAME **EVERY SINGLE DAY**, BRINGING MORE **FRUIT** THAN I COULD POSSIBLY **EAT**, AND YET LOOKING A LITTLE BIT MORE **NEGLECTED** EACH **TIME**. ON **CHRISTMAS DAY**, AFTER SHE'D GIVEN ME A LOVELY **SILK HAIR RIBBON** (MY HAIR'S GETTING **LONG** AGAIN), I ASKED WHY SHE DIDN'T **DRESS UP** SO MUCH NOW. SHE WOULDN'T LOOK AT ME FOR A BIT, BUT THEN ADMITTED TO ME **(A)**, THAT SHE WAS CONVINCED THAT ALL THIS WAS **HER** FAULT SOMEHOW, THAT SHE FELT SO **GUILTY** SHE JUST SAT **AWAKE** DAY & NIGHT **MOPING** UNTIL IT WAS **VISITING TIME** AGAIN (AND **THEN** THE NURSES PRACTICALLY HAD TO **THROW** HER OUT WHEN IT WAS **OVER**) ; AND THAT **(B)**, SHE WAS MISSING **HOME**.

I TOLD HER NOT TO BLAME **HERSELF** : THAT I **FELL** 'COS I WAS **PISSED**, AND I WAS **PISSED** 'COS I **DRANK** TOO MUCH — **END OF STORY**. **I ALSO** REASSURED HER THAT AS SOON AS I WAS **FIXED** I WOULD BE **LOOKING OUT** FOR HER, NOT TO **WORRY**, BLAH BLAH BLAH... I SHOULD HAVE BEEN AN **AGONY AUNT !** SHE **SPRUCED UP** A LOT AFTER THAT. I'M **SURE** SHE WAS **EXAGGERATING** ABOUT **STAYING AWAKE** ALL THAT TIME, THOUGH. THEY **SAY** YOU GO **BANANAS** IF YOU STAY AWAKE A **WEEK** ... THAT WOULD EXPLAIN A **LOT** IN **HER CASE !**

SO IN **BETWEEN** TIMES, "**ZIGGY PLAYED GUITAR**". I DIDN'T HAVE MY **TUTOR BOOK** WITH ME, AND I WAS ON THE **VERGE** OF ASKING **PANDA** TO BRING IT, BUT I FOUND IT MORE **FUN** TO IMAGINE FAMOUS **CHORDS** FROM **TUNES** AND TRY TO FIND THEM BY **EAR** — FOR INSTANCE, "**JILTED JOHN**" ONLY NEEDS **TWO** MOSTLY, THAT ONE WAS **EASY**. THE **FUNNY THING WAS**, I REALISED **THEN** THAT I WAS ACTUALLY **CONCENTRATING. MOST** OF THE TIME I'M TRYING TO JUGGLE **FIFTEEN THINGS** AT **ONCE** IN MY HEAD : **COURSEWORK**, **THESIS** IDEAS, **T.V.** SCHEDULES, **PARANOIA**, **DAYDREAMS**, HALF-WRITTEN **SCRIPTS**, YOU **NAME IT**. **BUT**, NOW THAT I HAD NOTHING TO **WORRY** ABOUT EXCEPT GETTING **BETTER** (WHICH PRETTY MUCH DOES **ITSELF**) AND PASSING THE **TIME**, I HAD **REDISCOVERED** SOMETHING I NEVER REALLY **NOTICE** MUCH - I'M **CLEVER** AS **HELL !** I KEPT FINDING **CHORD** AFTER **CHORD**, UP AND DOWN THE NECK, WRITING THE **HAND POSITIONS** DOWN UNTIL I RAN OUT OF **PAPER !** IN **SHORT**, I WAS A **NATURAL !** I MUST HAVE HAD '**PERFECT PITCH**' TOO - I DIDN'T KNOW PEOPLE **WEREN'T** SUPPOSED TO BE ABLE TO **IMAGINE** A CHORD AND PRISE EACH **NOTE** OUT OF IT STRAIGHT OFF. BY THE **30TH**, I WAS SO **HOT** I COULD TELL THAT THE **GUITARISTS** ON THE "**TOP OF THE POPS No. 1's OF THE YEAR**" SHOW ON **T.V.** WERE **MIMING** - THEY WEREN'T **PLAYING** THE SAME CHORDS I WAS **HEARING** (BUT NO SURPRISE **THERE !**)

HEAVEN KNOWS WHAT LEVELS MY **EGO** WOULD HAVE REACHED IF THAT WASN'T THE DAY I **FINALLY GOT OUT** ...

ANDIAMO!
RIGHT, IF YOU JUST PUT YOUR LEG UP HERE...
UH - HUH
NOW LET'S SEE - TWIST... PULL... LOOP IT AROUND... THAT GOES BEHIND THERE...
ERM, YOU DO ACTUALLY KNOW HOW TO DO THIS, I SUPPOSE?
OH YES - I JUST GO SLOWLY, THAT'S ALL...
RIGHT, THAT'S THAT ONE TIED UP - - THIS IS FUN! - NOW GIVE ME YOUR OTHER FOOT...
?
?
OH, HI! LOOK AT ME, MA- -TOP OF THE WORLD!
HULLO
HUP- THERE NOW...
-WE WERE WONDERING WHAT YOU WERE DOING IN THERE!
OH, SANDRA WAS JUST DOING UP MY SHOES FOR ME - I'M A BIT TOO STIFF TO REACH THEM JUST NOW...
OKAY THEN - WE'RE ALL READY FOR YOU WITH THE CAR. HAVE YOU GOT EVERYTHING PACKED?
YUP- ALL DONE.
-COULD YOU GET MY BAG PLEASE, PANDA?
HERE IT IS...
... I SUPPOSE THIS IS GOODBYE THEN?
WELL, NOW...
MUUUUM... YOU KNOW, SANDRA'S BEEN SOOO HELPFUL COMING IN AND BRINGING ALL THE ORANGES AND THINGS, WELL, I WAS WONDERING, SORT OF, IF YOU'D LET HER COME AND STAY WITH US FOR A BIT - -AS A SORT OF A "THANK YOU" AND STUFF...
BAT BAT
OH, JO, I'D LOVE TO NORMALLY, BUT WE'VE GOT THE WHOLE FAMILY STAYING - WHERE WOULD WE PUT HER?
awww pleeazze!..
- sigh - OKEY DOKEY- I'LL JUST HAVE TO TEAR UP MY DIAGRAM AND DO A NEW ONE!..
OOH, THANKS, MUM!
THERE, PANDA- WADJA THINKA THAT?!..
BLECH! SPEWOSITY UPTHROW!..

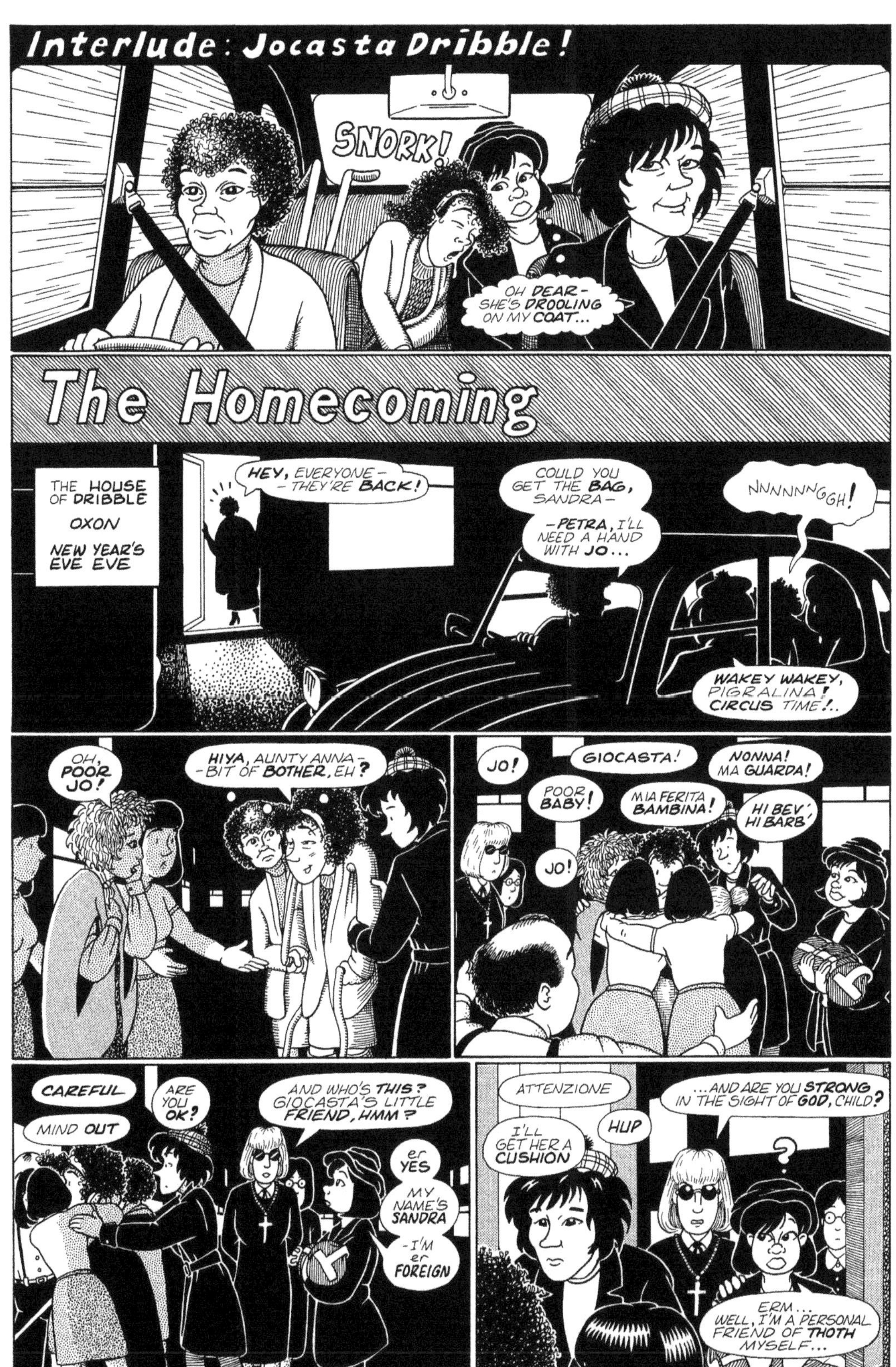
Interlude: Jocasta Dribble!
SNORK!
OH DEAR- SHE'S DROOLING ON MY COAT...
The Homecoming
THE HOUSE OF DRIBBLE
OXON
NEW YEAR'S EVE EVE
HEY, EVERYONE- -THEY'RE BACK!
COULD YOU GET THE BAG, SANDRA-
-PETRA, I'LL NEED A HAND WITH JO...
NNNNNNGGH!
WAKEY WAKEY, PIGRALINA! CIRCUS TIME!..
OH, POOR JO!
HIYA, AUNTY ANNA- -BIT OF BOTHER, EH?
JO!
GIOCASTA!
NONNA! MA GUARDA!
POOR BABY!
MIA FERITA BAMBINA!
HI BEV' HI BARB'
JO!
CAREFUL
MIND OUT
ARE YOU OK?
AND WHO'S THIS? GIOCASTA'S LITTLE FRIEND, HMM?
er YES
MY NAME'S SANDRA
-I'M er FOREIGN
ATTENZIONE
I'LL GET HER A CUSHION
HUP
...AND ARE YOU STRONG IN THE SIGHT OF GOD, CHILD?
?
ERM... WELL, I'M A PERSONAL FRIEND OF THOTH MYSELF...

THERE NOW
ECCO
LOVELY
TA, EVERYONE!
IS THAT NICE?
LET'S MAKE HER A CUPPA COFFEE...
AHEM! - COULD I HAVE YOUR ATTENTION A MOMENT?...
...THIS IS JO'S FRIEND SANDRA, AND SHE'S COME TO STAY WHILE JO'S RECOVERING...
HMM?
OH?
PREGO?
PARDON?
HELLO!
HELLO!
- NOW, WITH AN EXTRA GUEST, IT MEANS WE'LL HAVE TO MOVE ROUND A BIT, SO I JUST WANT TO AIR MY NEW SLEEPING PLAN FIRST, IN CASE ANYBODY OBJECTS, O.K?...
OH
OH
O.K.
SURE
ANNA, GIOVANNI, AND BARBARA'S BOYFRIEND MARLON STAY WHERE THEY ARE, IN THE CARAVAN...
DAMN!
CHRISTINA, BRUNO & THERESA ARE STILL IN PETRA'S ROOM...
JO GOES IN HER OWN ROOM, OF COURSE...
THAT MEANS BEVERLEY AND BARBARA SHIFT IN WITH ME AND NONNA FRANCESCA...
BAGS I THE BED!
CHE DICE?
NO! I HAD THE FLOOR LAST NIGHT - - BAGS ME!
...WHICH LEAVES PETRA AND SANDRA TO PICK BETWEEN THE SETTEE AND JO'S FLOOR, I'M AFRAID.
HMM- BEST KEEP THE 'BEANS' APART!
YOU CAN HAVE THE COMFY SOFA, SANDRA- -I'LL TAKE THE COLD HARD FLOOR!
OH, THANK YOU- - IF THAT'S ALL RIGHT, I MEAN...
BBC
RIGHT!! - NOW THAT THAT'S SORTED - ALL HANDS TO THE KITCHEN! WE'VE A HOMECOMING CELE-BRATION SUPPER TO COOK!..
KRAK
YUM!
OH BOY!
SPLENDID!
COME ON THEN
OO!
ANDIAMO!

• Blow-out!

DISGRACEFUL- EATING WITHOUT OFFERING GRACE
MMM
YES. TRULY WE ARE IN SODOM.
?
...AT LAST I GET TO EAT!
...SO WHAT DO YOU WANT?
WELL... I DO LIKE CHEESE, COFFEE AND CAPPELLETTI, BUT NOT TURKEY, ORANGES AND RAVIOLI...
UN PO' PIÙ DI TACCHINO, PER FAVORE, BARA-BARA
SONO BEVERLEY, NONNA!

... HEY, JO- ANY IDEA WHAT'S WITH ALL THESE ORANGES?
OH-MUM MUST HAVE USED UP SOME OF THE ONES SANDRA BROUGHT ME IN HOSPITAL

DIDN'T SHE GET YOU ANYTHING ELSE? -A BUNCH OF TRADITIONAL GRAPES, MAYBE!
WELL- SHE DIDN'T KNOW IF I LIKED ANYTHING ELSE, AND I DIDN'T LIKE TO COMPLAIN...

HEY! PANDA HASN'T SEEN THE GRISSINI TRICK, HAS SHE?
URGHH PETRA!! -NOT THE GRISSINI TRICK- IT'S GROSS!
OH?
NAH, NAH-
LOOK- ONE ORDINARY GRISSINO...

NNNGHH!
OOH, VERY GOOD- -I'VE SEEN IT DONE WITH A SWORD BEFORE, BUT NOT ONE OF THOSE...
!
BLEAAGGHH!!!

...WHEN YOU'RE QUITE FINISHED!... - YOU CAN WASH IT DOWN WITH SOME OF THE WINE YOU FORGOT TO BRING IN!
OH SHISH! (MUNCH MUNCH) "SISTER MINOR CLEAN-BOWLED BY SISTER MAJOR IN BOOZE AMNESIA HORROR!"
JUST A MO...
IS THIS SPECIAL CHRISTMAS FOOD, THEN?
WELL, IT'S WHAT ITALIANS HAVE FOR CHRISTMAS - WHICH IS BASICALLY THE SAME AS ANY OTHER DAY (BUT TWICE AS MUCH) PLUS A TURKEY!
JO'S ALREADY GOT ME HOOKED ON ITALIAN FOOD - - I LOVE PIZZA!
PIZZA, EH? WHICH RESTAURANT DID SHE TAKE YOU TO?..
OH, IT WAS THE HUTLAND-MMPH!
NOW YOU'VE DONE IT!...
HUTLAND!? JO-CASTA! WHAT MUCK HAVE YOU BEEN FEEDING THIS POOR GIRL?
oh gawd
YOU JUST SIT THERE, SANDRA - I SHOW YOU SOME REAL FOOD...
???
...HAVE A TASTE OF THAT!
?
- S'GOOD, EH?
?!
MM
NOD NOD NOD NOD
...HUTLAND?! JO'S POOR PAPA WOULD BE TURNING IN HIS GRAVE IF HE KNEW... ... NOW TRY SOME OF THIS...
= sigh = SHE'LL BE ON ABOUT THIS FOR DAYS, NOW...
??!!
OH - MIND THE ORANGES, MARLON!..

Goodbye Girl / Henry V / Happy New Year

-RIGHT! BIG COATS ON - IT'S TIME TO SHOW YOU SOME PRIMAEVAL LOCAL NEW YEAR'S CUSTOMS!
WHERE ARE WE GOING?
...THE PRIMAEVAL LOCAL PUB OF COURSE!

BYE, JO! SORRY YOU COULDN'T MAKE IT - WE'LL BRING YOU BACK A PACKET OF CRISPS, EH?
SENZ'ALTRO! TATA!
NNUUHH...
-AND YOU REMEMBER- YOU HAVE TO KEEP AN EYE ON SANDRA FOR ME!
BYE

SOME TIME LATER...
= Yawn =
OH, I THINK I'LL SKIP 'HOGMANAY' THIS YEAR, I'M TOO TIRED...
KNOCK KNOCK!
-THAT'LL BE THEM BACK...

HULLO! -HAPPY NEW FOOT! -OR IS IT HAPPY FIRST YEAR?
?
OH? -WHERE'S PETRA?

...OH, SHE SAID SHE WAS GOING TO HENRY'S PARTY. I TOLD HER I WAS A BIT WARY OF PARTIES THESE DAYS, SO SHE GOT ME THIS TAXI TO TAKE ME BACK HERE.
HENRY, EH? HMM -SHE SHOULD BE ALL RIGHT AT HIS HOUSE... -HE'S A GOOD BOY, I LIKE HIM...

OKEY DOKE, I'M OFF NOW- -KEEP THE T.V. DOWN LOW AND MAKE SURE TO LOCK UP AFTER PETRA GETS IN. -SEE YOU IN THE MORNING!..
BYE
BYE MUM

"HENRY" EH? ANOTHER HENRY - FIVE IN A ROW...HUMMM...
WHAT DO YOU MEAN, "ANOTHER HENRY"?

...WELL, TO BE HONEST, SHE HASN'T SEEN HENRY IN MONTHS - IT'S JUST HER EXCUSE WHEN SHE'S OFF ON THE TILES WITH HER LATEST "HUNK"...
OH?

...LET'S JUST HOPE SHE TOOK 'JOHNNY' WITH HER AS WELL!
WHO'S HE?
-NEVER MIND...

EGGS and BACON
WHAT'S THE NATIONAL CAKE OF BAVARIA?
DON'T KNOW.
WHAT'S THE 'B' SIDE OF "DON'T BE CRUEL"?
NOPE.
WHAT'S TARZAN'S REAL NAME?
NOT A CLUE.
HMM... I DON'T THINK WE'RE GOING TO GET VERY FAR WITH THIS!...
SLAM!
HOWDY GELS! -CATCH!
HIYA- -OOH!...
JANUARY 5TH? -MUST BE SOME SORT OF RECORD!
EH? WHAT RECORD?
?
-THE RECORD FOR THE EARLIEST EASTER EGGS IN THE SHOPS! -AND TALKING OF RECORDS, I HAVEN'T PUT WAGNER ON TODAY, HAVE I? -CIAO CIAO!
BYE
UH-OH! NOT WAGNER AGAIN! EVERY SINGLE DAY SINCE SHE GOT IT THAT'S BEEN ON...
-WE NEED TO ESCAPE!
HEY! I COULD TAKE YOU OUT IN THE GARDEN AND-
-uggh- NO I COULDN'T COULD I?
KLIK!
WHAT?
...I COULD HAVE TAKEN YOU OUT AND SHOWED YOU HOW TO BUILD A SNOWMAN -BUT FOR THESE CHIMNEY POTS ON MY LEGS, THAT IS!...
MONOPOLY"
nington Cresc
Stump?!
CIVILIZ
OH DEAR- OF COURSE.
THAT'S A SHAME... MAYBE I COULD DO IT MYSELF IF YOU COACHED ME FROM IN HERE.
Hmm hmm hmm hmm hmm hmm HMMMMM!...
HMM... WHY NOT? -WE'LL FINISH THESE CHOCCY EGGS FIRST, THOUGH!!...

BY THE **WAY** – SEE THAT BIG **STONE** OUT THERE? IT'S SOME SORT OF **NEOLITHIC** THINGY – **THOUSANDS** OF YEARS OLD. I DON'T KNOW WHAT IT'S DOING AT THE BOTTOM OF **OUR** GARDEN, THOUGH – – THEY MUST'VE JUST BUILT THE ESTATE **ROUND IT**.

Woglinde, wachst du allein?

Mit Wellgunde war ich zu zwei

HMM... I'M NOT **SURE**, BUT I THINK OUR **ENTIRE HOUSE** BACK HOME IS BUILT OF STONE LIKE THAT

"**BACK HOME**" HMMMM...

... WHAT'S IT LIKE IN **THAILAND**? I BET IT'S **LOVELY** OVER THERE AT THE MOMENT.

Lass' seh'n wie du wachst

Sicher vor dir

ERM, **YES, WELL**, I DON'T KNOW IF YOU'D **LIKE** IT – – IT'S SORT OF LIKE A **WHOLE DIFFERENT WORLD**!?..

HEIAHA WEIA! WILDES GESCHWISTER!

PETRA! NOT SO **LOUD**!

–AND **WHY** CAN'T YOU PLAY SOME **PUCCINI**, FOR HEAVEN'S SAKE! YOUR **PAPA** WOULD BE TURNING IN HIS **GRAVE**...

AW, "**DISPY ATCHY**," MA!...

KLIK

PHEW! S' **BETTER**!...

SO **ANYWAY**, TELL ME ABOUT YOUR **HOUSE**, THEN – – IT'S PRETTY **BIG**, ISN'T IT?

BIG?

YOU WANT TO KNOW HOW **BIG** IT IS??

IT'S **SO BIG**, THAT...

... **BACK** WHEN I WAS **TINY**, I USED TO WANDER ALL OVER THE HOUSE AND GROUNDS, AND I KEPT GETTING **LOST**...

... MY **NURSE** HAD THE IDEA OF TYING A BIT OF **STRING** AROUND MY WAIST SO THAT I COULD **FOLLOW IT BACK**...

... SHE WOULD ALSO **TUG** ON IT AT **MEALTIMES**.

BY THE TIME I WAS **EIGHT**, HOWEVER, I WAS GETTING A BIT **SICK** OF THIS.

WELL **ONE** DAY, NURSE TUGGED ON THE **STRING** AND GOT **NO RESPONSE**, SO SHE **FOLLOWED** THE STRING TO ITS **END**.

... UH **HUH**.

- SO DID SHE **FIND** YOU?

EVENTUALLY- AFTER THEY GOT HER **DOWN** FROM THE **TREE**!...

epilogue: "I've been makin' a man..."

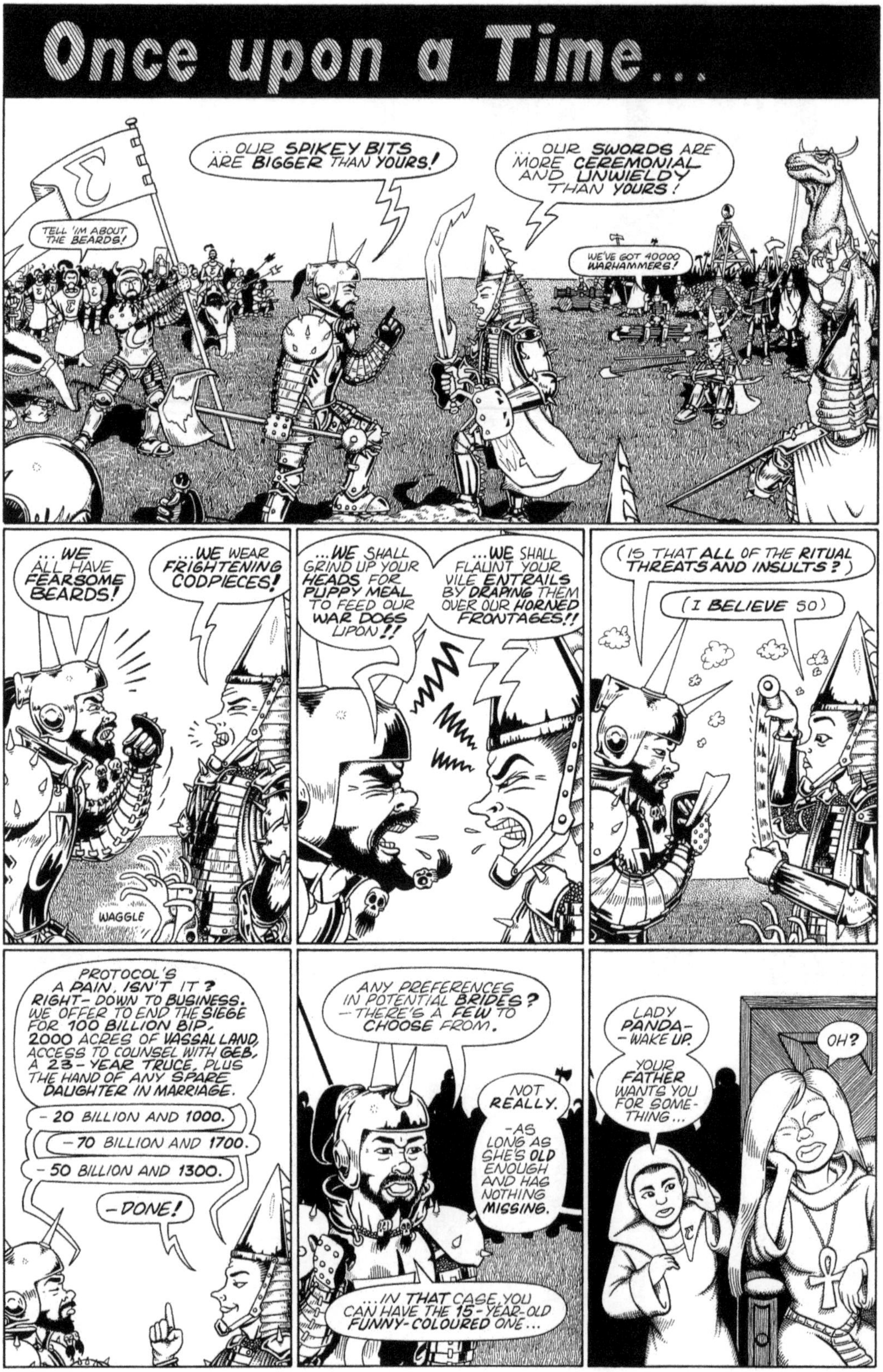

Once upon a Time...

Bus Thinks

NNNGGH... ...CAN'T GET COMFY ON THIS HEADREST... ...WHOEVER DESIGNED IT MUST BE SOME SORT OF PSYCHO...
...MY CALF'S ITCHY AGAIN... ...CAN'T BE BOTHERED TO REACH IT... ...KNITTING NEEDLE'S IN THE BAG ANYWAY...
...MUST GET ROUND TO THE HOSPITAL AND GET THOSE STUPID CRUTCHES CHANGED, THEY'RE TOTALLY USELESS...
...IT'LL BE THE WOMEN CARTOONISTS SOCIETY MEETING ON THE 24TH, S'POSE I'D BETTER GO TO THAT...
...NO POINT BOTHERING THE DRAMA SOC. LOT 'TIL THE 'POTS' ARE OFF...
...CAN'T WAIT TO GET BACK ON THE 'AXE' AGAIN... HAVE A BASH AT SOME SIOUXSIE STUFF, MAYBE... ..."VOIIICE-ES, FROM THE AIIIRRR"... ...VERITY USED TO SING THAT ONE... ...WONDER WHAT SHE'S DOING THESE DAYS...
- OH YES, MUST FINISH OFF THAT PAPER ON 'BLOCKBUSTERS' ...WELL, START IT ANYWAY... ...MAYBE NEXT WEEK...
...HAVE TO GET PANDA TO STICK UP A NOTE CANCELLING THE TUTORIAL TOO - - CAN'T BE ARSED TO HOBBLE UP TO FLOOR 6 AND WITTER ON ABOUT "SYMBOL AND JUXTAPOSITION" JUST YET...
...URGH, I WAS SUPPOSED TO REVISE THE NOTES FOR IT OVER THE HOLS ANYWAY... ...TOO MUCH FAFFING ABOUT WITH PANDA AND THE FOLKS... ...HOPE 'BAR' AND 'MAR' DON'T SET THEIR WEDDING IN HOLS TIME, I'D HAVE TO GO, AND I'D ONLY MAKE A SCENE WEEPING AGAIN... SIGH...
...WONDER WHEN THE HOT CHOCOLATE WOMAN'S COMING ROUND AGAIN, I COULD DO WITH SOME MORE... ...MAYBE NOT - MRS. BLADDER'S WHINGEING ABOUT THE LAST TWO ALREADY!...
...SEE IF THEY'VE GOT THE MATCHING LEGGINGS AND HEADBAND... ...AND MAYBE THREE OR FOUR MORE SWEATERS, TWO BLACK, RED FOR THE ANORAK AND MAYBE A GREEN ONE FOR CONTRAST...
...HEAVEN KNOWS HOW I'LL GET ALL THIS STUFF HOME - I'D NEED A TROLLEY!...
...SHOULD BE ABOUT NINETY DAYS 'TIL I GET BACK... AND ONLY FIVE MINUTES PASSED OVER THERE... ...STRAIGHT IN THE BIG BATH, I RECKON... BE HEAVENLY COMPARED TO THAT HALLS ONE YOU CAN BARELY LIE STRAIGHT OUT IN...
...AT LEAST I CAN GET MADE UP WITHOUT SNEAKING ABOUT, NOW...
...THAT CHRISTINA WOMAN NEARLY CAUGHT ME, ONCE...
...WONDER WHY SHE WEARS THOSE DARK GLASSES ALL THE TIME...
...LIKED THE OTHER RELATIVES BETTER, THOUGH... ...THE FRIENDLY TWINS... ...THAT PETRA REMINDS ME OF EBIRA, THE WAY SHE TEASED JO... ...NEARLY AS POTTY AS GIDRA WAS, TOO...
...I SUPPOSE I LOOK A LOT LIKE EBIRA, NOW, IN MY DISGUISE...
...I MISS HER, EVEN THOUGH SHE WAS MEAN TO ME...
...GIDRA WOULD HAVE ENDED UP LOOKING LIKE I NORMALLY DO, IF SHE'D REACHED THE RIGHT AGE... HER EYES WERE ROYAL BLUE INSTEAD OF PINK, OF COURSE... HAIR WAS MORE GOLDEN THAN FLAT WHITE, TOO...
...I WISH I COULD SLEEP, SO I COULD DREAM THEY WERE STILL HERE...
...A BIT DIFFICULT IN THIS TORTURE RACK OF A SEAT, THOUGH!...

Good Morning Vietgrove

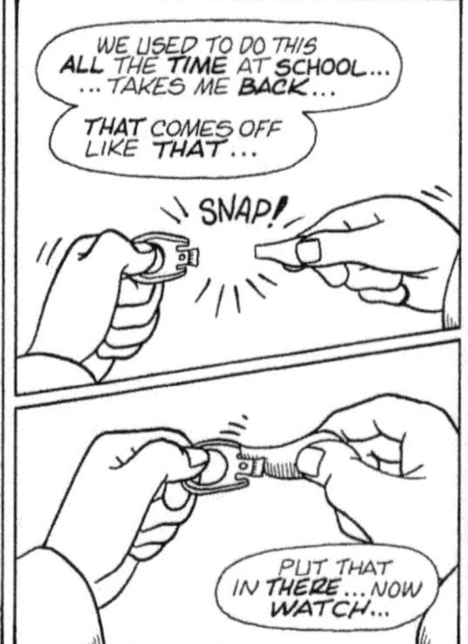

OOPS!
BOBBINS!
YELP!

TIME WE WERE ELSEWHERE, METHINKS!
EH?
WHAT'S THE MATTER, BOY?
DID YOU STEP ON A SHARP THING?
NE-VER MIND!...
?
ROOF!
!!

...I DON'T KNOW WHY YOU HAVE TO GO BY BUS - I'D HAVE PAID FOR A TAXI...
OH SHUSH!
GIMME SHELTER

WE WANNA BE FREE TO DO WHAT WE WANNA DO HAVE A GOOD TIME HAVE A PARTY

WHAT'S TH-
BLOODY HELL!
THERE IT IS!
C'MON!...
RRUMM!
?!

503
HANG ON! HANG ON!...
PANT! GASP!
FSSH
RUDDR RUDDR RUDDR

TWO =wheeze= FOR RED AWL DRIVE =wheeze= PLEASE!
PHEW!

ARE YOU OK?
SO FAR!
-S'LONG AS THE BUS DOESN'T-

LURCH!
RRRRUMMMMM!
OOOCH!!
-THAT'S A DOUBLE OOCH!

B'STARD BUS DRIVERS!...
..."YOU WON'T CATCH ME ON THE FIVE-OH-THREE!"
hee hee hee hee hee hee
A1089
COAST ROAD
SOON
YOU NEED A
WHOOPS-A-DAISY...
=GRUNT!=
PHEW!...
1068A
WELL- THIS IS THE PLACE-
-HOPE THE LIFT'S WORKING!...
← Exit
West Wing ↑
Main Building →
MAIN BUILDING
ACCORDING TO THIS NOTE IT ISN'T-
-WHAT FLOOR ARE WE GOING TO?
JUST THE FIRST, LUCKILY!
KITCHEN
MUMBLE MUTTER GRUNT!
...COULD YOU GET THE DOOR FOR ME, PLEASE?
CERTAINLY...

THERE YOU ARE...
=huff=
-TA.

HMM...
NOW, IS THIS THE HIGH NUMBERS END, OR THE—

YIPE!
SLIDE

-MORON!
THUD!

GRRNNGHH... SASSAFRASSIN' "SUICIDE MATS!"
HANG ON...
-WHICH ROOM IS IT?

...IT'S THIS 'UN
KNOCK
KNOCK
101
Dee
John
Come in!
COME IN!

HI, FOLKS!
...THIS IS PANDA - SHE'S COME ALONG TO HELP GET ME HERE!...
Hi, Jo
HI!
HELLO
'ALLO

Jo, this is Bea - she's just joined us
OH- HELLO!
Hiyuh, Jo!
Bea Dennehy-
- nice to meetcha

HEY, NEAT CAT!
RRRR
LASH
This is Odin - he's been poorly, so I brought him along
I'VE NOT SEEN YOU AROUND THE UNIVERSITY
-That's cos I'm down the road at the College of Arts and Tech - a "Mature Student"
C.A.T. EH? VERY APPROPRIATE!
TREAD TREAD
-SO HOW DID YOU FIND OUT ABOUT THE SOCIETY, THEN?
Well, I just contacted the address in the back of "Bog" comic, didn't I?
OH. YES, OF COURSE
NOW THEN, PANDA - THIS IS:
ROSIE SIMONS...
BEA, YOU'VE MET...
CAROLE DAY...
DENIS' JEROME...
DEE JOHN...
TIA McQUEEN...
AND JUDY de SADE
So, er...
PANDA
SO WHAT'S THE BIG TOPIC TODAY?
It's Tia and Dee's comic - - you know they've taken the plunge and published something 'proper'...
"Panda" - you involved with these guys?
ME? NO, I'M JUST TAGGING ALONG TO HELP JO
UH HUH - "THE FAR LOOK" ISN'T IT?
-WELL, WE'VE BROUGHT IN ALL OF THE MAGAZINES THAT REVIEWED IT, SO EVERYONE CAN HAVE A LOOK -
-AND THEY'RE ALL OVER THE PLACE!
-HAVE A LOOK AT THIS LOT...
Hmm... "THE CHARACTERS SAY WITTY THINGS TO EACH OTHER RATHER THAN EXHIBIT PERSONALITIES"
?
BUT THIS ONE SAYS: "THE DIALOGUE IS SHARPLY REALISTIC... ... CONVINCING AND OFTEN VERY FUNNY"...
"STIFF AND LABOURED INKING... MUCH TOO CLUTTERED... ... LACKS SPONTANEITY"
"Very clean style... attractive and seamless artwork... classically cute"
SEE WHAT I MEAN?

This one doesn't like it because it isn't Matt Howarth
But this one says "Like a cuddlier Matt Howarth"
"THE STORY IS KEPT BRIGHT AND ENTERTAINING"
But it's "fairly difficult to follow what's going on"
-LOOKS LIKE WE CAN'T WIN!

I guess you should have expected that - I mean, they're all by different people with differing tastes.
BULLSHIT-THEY JUST DON'T KNOW WHAT TO MAKE OF A COMIC IF IT ISN'T MAINSTREAM!
Fair's fair, though - without a mainstream to react against, there wouldn't BE a W.C.S, would there?

ERM, EXCUSE ME...
Yeah?
-WHY DO YOU HAVE A SOCIETY JUST FOR WOMEN? -JO TOLD ME THERE'S A "KOMIK KLUB", ISN'T THERE?

Well YES - but have you SEEN it? I mean - -the name says it ALL doesn't it?
I DON'T KNOW - -DOES IT?

-THE KOMIK KLUB'S 95% FULL OF STEREOTYPICAL COMIC READERS...
-THAT'S TO SAY PIMPLY, GEEKY BOYS GETTING EXCITED OVER ENDLESS, MINDLESS SAGAS ABOUT SUPER-HEROES IN TIGHT COSTUMES

-AND A FEMALE COMIC READER (OR CREATOR) IS A BIG NOVELTY FOR THEM!
-THEY WERE ALWAYS PESTERING US - DESPERATE FOR GIRLFRIENDS!
...Never thinking that we might not be particularly interested!

So we started the Women Cartoonist Society so that we could do stories about, well, everything else! Stuff we're into... that doesn't just mean Feminist tracts, or promoting some kind of lesbian agenda, though

'COURSE NOT - I MEAN, WE DO SCIENCE FICTION, FOR INSTANCE...
STRICTLY SPEAKING, OUGHTN'T WE TO BE EITHER THE WOMAN CARTOONISTS OR THE WOMEN'S CARTOONIST SOCIETY?
?

THREE NIGHTS LATER, THE "KOMIK KLUB" HAVE *THEIR* MEETING...

* COMING SOON FROM "FIGHT-SCENE" COMIX! (PERHAPS)

'diary of a lost girl'

Monday Feb. 2nd – Haven't seen Panda all day...
CLICK
– So put your liddle hand in mine, Together there's no mountain we can't climb...
(doo doo doo) doo PAPAA doo PAPAA
I got you babe, I got you babe...
– TELL ME WHY!
AH DON'T LIKE MON-DAYS
TELL ME WHY!
AH DON'T LIKE MO-ON-DAYS...
Lazy bones, sleepin' in the sun...
MMM...
THE BEST THING ABOUT BEING A FAKE STUDENT...
... IS NEVER HAVING TO GET UP AND GO TO LECTURES – EVER!...
Sat. Feb 14th – no comment!
DUNGGG DUNGA DUNG DUNGA DUNGA DUNGG DUNGGG
CAAM ONNN DAOWN! THE PRIIIICE IZZ RIIIIGHT!
CLAP CLAP CLAP CLAP CLAP CLAP
(sigh)
IF SOMEONE DOESN'T SHOVE A VALENTINE UNDER THAT DOOR SOON, I COULD START GETTING DEPRESSED!..
Tuesday Feb. 17th – Halls food's getting worse...
UGH – STICKY PUDDING AGAIN!
– ROLL ON SHROVE TUESDAY!
WHY?
'COS THAT'S PANCAKE DAY
– WE GET TO EAT PANCAKES INSTEAD OF THE USUAL MUCK
OH RIGHT.
– BUT WHAT'S A SHROVE?
ERM – I'M NOT SURE
WELL MAYBE IT'S A PANCAKE THEN.
Saturday Feb 21st – "Free of costs, free of costs great God almighty, we are free of costs!!!!!"

Spend, Spend, Spend!

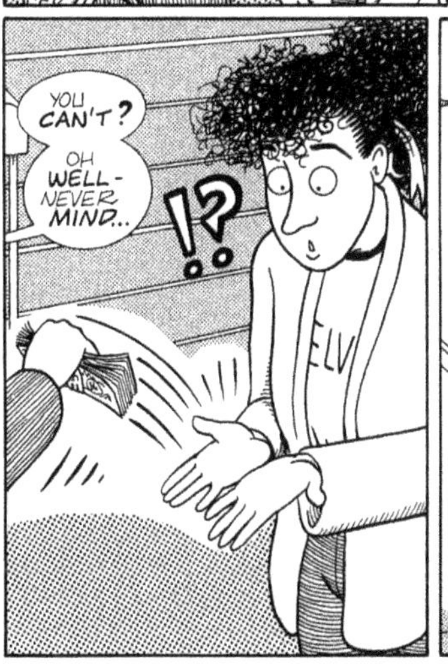

LATER
FORGOTTEN PELMET BOOX COMIX & RECORDZ
...SO EVEN IF THE BLOKE'S, LIKE, KISSING YOU, THAT STILL MEANS ZIP, REALLY
...I WISH I'D ASKED ABOUT THIS SOONER - I COULD HAVE RISKED GOING TO THAT PARTY WITH PETRA AND HER FRIENDS

...WELL, I DON'T THINK THERE EVER WAS A PARTY- -SHE WAS PROBABLY JUST TRYING TO DUMP YOU GENTLY SO SHE COULD GO OFF WITH A BLOKE - LIKE I SAID, PETRA SWITCHES BLOKES WHENEVER SHE GETS TIRED OF THE LAST ONE.
YOU COULDN'T DO THAT IN MY COUNTRY - OR AT LEAST YOU COULDN'T WHEN I WAS A KID...

I DON'T APPROVE ANYWAY - SHE'S ASKING FOR TROUBLE, I RECKON...
...HMM...WHAT'S THIS?
OH- IS THIS THE 'DARK NIGHTWATCHMEN' EVERYONE'S TALKING ABOUT?...
TRAPPED IN A HUT HE NEVER MADE!
...SO YOU'D STICK WITH ONE MAN, THEN?

HMM?... OH, YEAH, I SUPPOSE... (sigh) CHANCE'D BE A FINE THING - I HAVEN'T BEEN OUT WITH A FELLER FOR Y- AGES. I'M CERTAINLY NO PARTY ANIMAL, AM I?...
SPONGE COMIC
OH JO, YOU'RE PATHETIC! AT LEAST I'M EXCUSED FOR BEING IGNORANT - YOU KNOW ALL THE RULES AND YOU STILL WON'T TRY!!
NNNGGHH...

...WOW! I'LL NEED TO BUY A NEW TAPE RACK FOR ALL THESE - ...HENDRIX...STONES... WHATSERNAME, SINEAD O'CONNOR...
I LIKE THIS THING! MY...
FIRST HUSBAND?...nah
...UNCLE USED TO HAVE ONE!
TAP TAP TAP TAP
TAP TAP TAP TAP - TL-AT
KCHING!
echo and the bunnymen

HEY - IT'S RAG WEEK SOON! -I FORGOT ALL ABOUT IT.
HUGIN SWEDA 1089
23.17
RaG Week PaRaDE
March 7th
PiaNo TAROWING
CLOG DANCING
CusTaRD FiLLED BOOT RACE
AT THE PERPETUAL RISK OF SOUNDING DUMB- -WHAT'S RAG WEEK?

...IT'S WHEN STUDENTS DRESS UP IN FUNNY COSTUMES AND STUFF, AND DO CRAZY STUNTS FOR CHARITY
NOW THAT SOUNDS LIKE FUN!
-WHAT SORT OF THINGS DO THEY DO?

-THEY SHAKE TINS AND SELL RAG MAGAZINES AND...
AHHHHHH, NOW- -I'M HAVING AN IDEA!...
OHHH?

STORE TREK : THE SEARCH FOR TAT!

'FUNNY COSTUMES'

ACCESSORIES

BIGGER AMPLIFIER...

...MORE SOUNDS

TRANSPORT

...RIGHT, YOU MIGHT WANT TO LISTEN TO SOME OF THESE, - I'LL LEND YOU MY GHETTO BLASTER TOO - OH POOH, I NEVER BOUGHT THOSE JEANS, UM, COULD I BORROW THOSE CHINO'S OF YOURS - HAVE TO GET IN SOME HEAVY DUTY GUITAR PRACTISE NEXT WEEK, WE'LL NEED A HAT, TOO - HOPE THE WEATHER DOESN'T TURN COLD AGAIN - 'COURSE YOU'LL HAVE TO CARRY THE AMP, SEEING AS MY LEGS ARE STILL OFFICIALLY FRAGILE - HAVE TO BUNG SOME MONEY IN THE HAT FIRST, OF COURSE, SO IT DOESN'T LOOK AS IF WE'RE UTTERLY RUBBISH...
blah blah blah...

...THE GIRL'S POSESSED!

...AND FINALLY

RAG 'n' ROCK!

GUITAR TUNED UP!
CHECK!

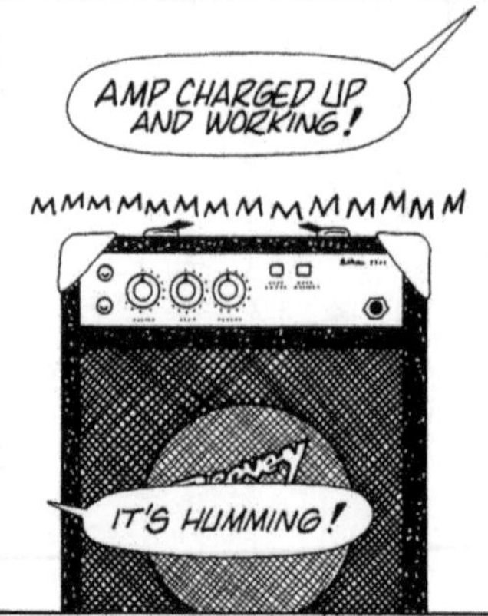
AMP CHARGED UP AND WORKING!
MMMMMMMMMMMMMMMMM
IT'S HUMMING!

FLOAT FOR BUSK HAT!
ONE POUND THIRTY EIGHT PENCE!

CHECK BANDANNA!
SMART!

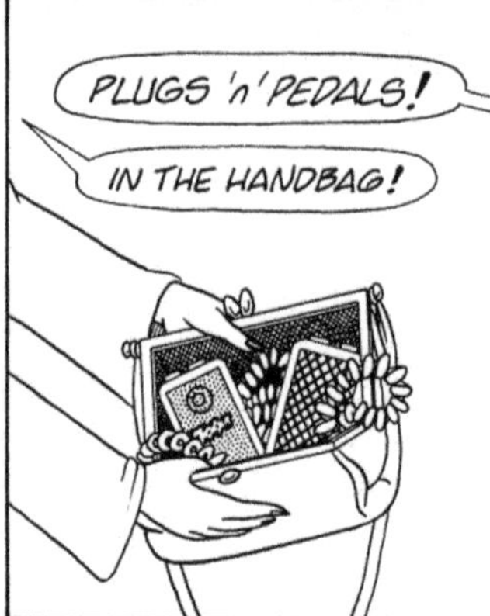
PLUGS 'n' PEDALS!
IN THE HANDBAG!

CHECK GARISH DANCE OUTFIT!
NAUSEATING!
RIGHT – IF THAT'S EVERYTHING...

-LET'S ROCK!
MMMMMMM

going places

Performance

the bride wore black

NNOOO... GOTHIC... GOTHIC- -NEAREST I KNOW IS 'SIOUXSIE AND THE BANSHEES'- -"FIREWORKS"?
OY!
YEAH, SMASHIN'!
-CHUCK US YER "A"...

SHAKE SHAKE SHAAKE
WOO OO WO OO WOOOH
CHUGA DA CHUNG
WE ARE FIREWORKS

SEVERAL SONGS LATER
AYYY THANK YOW!
THANNGK YEEOWW!
CLAP CLAP CLAP CLAP-CLAP

PHEW! I'M KNACKERED! I THINK IT MUST BE TIME FOR A LUNCH BREAK
YEAH, TOO RIGHT- RECKON AH COULD DO WI' A CUPPA FOR ME THROAT

CAFE KIRKBY
'KNACKERED' - A NEW WORD. MEANS 'TIRED' I BET!
Y'NOT WRONG! NEW WORD, EH?
DON'T MIND HER- SHE'S FOREIGN...
OPEN

THERE Y'GO
...NOW LET ME GET THIS STRAIGHT- YOU PLAY MUSIC THEN GIVE PEOPLE MONEY?
YEAH...

...BUT I THOUGHT THE IDEA OF BUSKING WAS TO RAISE MONEY.
WELL, YEAH, USUALLY. THIS IS MORE OF A...ER, ANNIVERSARY THING.
-YOU DO THIS EVERY YEAR?

YEAH, RAG WEEK.
EACH YEAR I, ERR...

MMMM?

the man who fell to earth

...I ONLY MADE OUT I WERE A GOTH AT FIRST—EXCUSE TO KEEP THE FROCK—THEN I FOUND I'D BEEN MEKKIN' OUT SO LONG I GOT TO LIKE IT FOR REAL.
—THERE NOW, THAT'S HOW AH BECOME THE WOMAN I AM TODAY!

...OKAY, THAT'S YER LOT! YOU CAN DRINK YER TEA NOW—IF IT AIN'T COLD BY NOW, THAT IS!
UHHHHH...

LATER
REET, THEN—AH'VE GOT TONS MORE TENPENCES TO SHIFT TODAY, SO I'LL BE OFF—SEE YOUS TWO ROUND THE UNI SOME TIME, EH? TARRAH!
ERR... RIGHT. OKAY. BYE!.
BLURRGH—CREEPY?

67
...YES, BUT INTERESTING, TOO. SHAME SHE COULDN'T JOIN—
—HEY, LOOK!
WHAT? —OH, BRILLIANT—OUR PITCH HAS BEEN TAKEN!...

—WHO ARE THEY?
SPONSORED POSERS—YOU GIVE 'EM A POUND AND THEY DO YOU A HEROIC POSE TO STIRRING MUSIC—'TANNHAUSER', I THINK THAT IS—BLOODY WAGNER AGAIN!..
PAM PAAAM! PAM PAAM PAPAPA PAAM PAAM PAPAA PAAM PAM PAAAM!

WELL, WE CAN'T BUSK HERE NOW—WE'LL HAVE TO FIND SOMEWHERE ELSE...
C'MON THEN—TOTE SOME BARGES—I'VE AN IDEA FOR ANOTHER GOOD SPOT...

RAILWAY STATION
...THE RAILWAY STATION! WE CAN CATCH ALL THE PEOPLE GETTING OFF TRAINS, SEE?
—NICE ACOUSTIC TOO.
WHY YES—GOOD THINKING, JO!

HERE—YOU KNOW THAT SINEAD O'CONNOR TAPE I JUST BOUGHT? IT'S GOT THIS SONG ON IT I REALLY LIKE—SEE IF YOU CAN GUESS WHY!.
OKAY.

...I SAY, DON'T CALL ME LADYYY, JUST CALL ME JO, DON'T CALL ME MISTERRR, JUST CALL ME JO, DON'T CALL ME SWEETHEARRRT, (DOO DOO DOO) —JUST CALL ME JO!
dung Dung DUNG dung Dung DUNG dung Dung DUNG

OOH, VERY GOOD! A SONG JUST FOR YOU!...
THOUGHT YOU'D LIKE IT!...
CLAP CLAP
HEY!

HEY YOU THERE, BUSKING!
WHAT IS IT?
I DON'T KNOW, BUT I THINK WE'RE ON ITS PATCH! -ERM, JUST GRAB EVERYTHING AND WALK AWAY CASUALLY!...

C'MON JO!
OH NOOO, I CAN'T RUN, MY LEGS ARE STILL STIFF!...
STOP! COME BACK!

AAAAGH!!!
LUNGE

GRR!
NO, WAIT JO, LOOK!
ALL RIGHT! WE'RE SORRY! YOU CAN HAVE THE MONEY JUST DON'T HIT ME, O.K.?

THER-EEESA!!! IT'S YOU! WHA??-

JO'S COUSIN? BUH- -WHAT'S HAPPENED TO YOUR VOICE?
LA-RYN GI-TIS!
...BUT WHAT ARE YOU DOING HERE?

TOO LONG TO EXPLAIN— —HURTS!
WELL, DON'T JUST LIE THERE, JO! GET HER SOME-THING TO WRITE WITH!...
UNNGH!...

ONE PAD, PEN AND CHOCOLATE MILKSHAKE (OUT OF HAT FUNDS) LATER...
DON'T TRY TO TALK— JUST WRITE.
YEAH, AND KEEP SIPPING THAT SHAKE- -THAT'S MY PATENT SORE THROAT CURE!
Ive run away from home! my mother's been deceiving me all my Life!!!

She's not blind at all!!

SHE ISN'T?

No! I caught her reading an Agatha Christie in secret! Every day, she's had me leading her around, reading the Bible to her and stuff, and she can see as well as me! She's been pretending all this time!!!

BUT WHY SHOULD SHE DO THAT?

Teach me duty? Some sort of faith thing? e.g. St. Simeon Stylites sitting on top of a pillar for 45 years etc.? Don't ask me!

BUT WHAT ARE YOU DOING UP HERE?

I came to find YOU! I'm never going back! I would have gone to Uncle Joe's but I wanted to get as far away from Mother as possible.

- BUT WHY DIDN'T YOU COME STRAIGHT TO THE UNIVERSITY?

I did, I went there and they'd never heard of you

OH NO! YOU DIDN'T GO TO THE ONE STRAIGHT UP THIS ROAD, DID YOU?

yes

- THAT'S THE OTHER ONE! THAT'S JESSE HILL CAMPUS! WE'RE AT NOVOCASTRIA!

In the station, it was awful! some rotten thief stole my duffle bag with all my money in!

WHAAAT?!

OH NO! WHAT THEN?

It was getting dark and I was crying and an old tramp woman came asking what was wrong and I told her and she lent me some of her jumpers and stuff to keep warm and let me sleep in her cardboard box.

OH TERRY! YOU SHOULD HAVE GONE TO THE POLICE STRAIGHT AWAY!

Oh no! They'd only send me back to HER again!!!

-BUT YOU CAN'T STAY WITH ME - APART FROM IT'S NOT ALLOWED, YOUR MUM AND DAD WILL BE WORRIED MENTAL, RINGING THE POLICE AND THINGS. AND YOU'VE ALREADY GONE AND CAUGHT SOMETHING BY SLEEPING ROUGH!

My voice you mean? I ruined that in the Arcade yesterday, singing "Ave Maria" for money!

-DON'T CHANGE THE SUBJECT! YOU HAVE TO GO BACK YOU KNOW.

HutLand
THERE Y'GO, TERRY - SHAME THEY WON'T LET YOU IN LOOKING LIKE THAT
THANK YOU!
WHAT A CHEEK! - I CAN SEE WHY YOUR MOTHER LOATHES HUTLAND!
GARLIC BREAD
GARLIC BREAD
PIZZA SLICE

...PRETENDING TO BE BLIND?! WHAT A WEIRD TRICK TO PLAY ON YOUR OWN DAUGHTER.
IT'S ODD - NO ONE EVER ACTUALLY SAID SHE WAS BLIND - SHE'S ALWAYS HAD WEAK EYES, SO EVERYONE JUST ASSUMED THEY'D GOT WORSE - AND SHE NEVER THOUGHT TO TELL US OTHERWISE! - NO OFFENCE, TERRY, BUT AUNTY CHRISTINA'S GOT A PRETTY MEAN STREAK
NONE TAKEN (MUNCH) KNOW WHAT YOU MEAN

... LIKE THE TIME SHE CAME TO TELL ME PAPA HAD BEEN LOST AT SEA - SHE JUST CAME OUT AND SAID HE WAS DEAD - NOT 'GONE FOR A HOLIDAY WITH JESUS IN DADDY HEAVEN' OR ANYTHING, JUST DEAD - AND BURDENED WITH SIN TO BOOT!
OH, I DIDN'T KNOW - YOU NEVER SAID.
S'NO MATTER. S'A LONG TIME AGO NOW.

sigh ...I BAWLED AND BATTERED ANUBIS ON THE LEG WHEN MY MOTHER DIED, BUT HE STILL WOULDN'T LET ME SEE HER...
Y'KNOW, TERRY, I STILL HAVEN'T THE SLIGHTEST IDEA WHAT GOES ON IN HER HEAD!...
*?!@$

...YOU MUST REE NOUNCE THE GARB OF SAYTEN, CHILD! CAST HIM AOUWT!
DON'TCHOO START ON ME FLEMMIN' DRESS, NOW, Y'OLE GET!
WHAT THE- - OH-OH! IT'S THOSE FUNDAMENTALIST EVANGELISTS AGAIN!..

- CAN'T YOU SEE HOW SATAN HAS TWISTED YOUR MIND?
- AH'LL TWIST YER EAR IN A MINUTE!
HEY! WHAT'S GOING ON?

- 'MAH GLAD TO SEE YOUS AGAIN! - THIS BUGGER'S BIN FOLLOWIN' ME
- THAT'S HER, THE SATANIST!
HOWLY JEEZERS WHUT HAVE WE HERE? YER MULTI-COLOURED ACOLYTES IN SIN??
NOW, JUST WAIT A MINUTE!

- THIS CALLS FOR DRASTIC MEASURES - AH CALL UPON THE RAPTURE OF THE HOWLY SPEERET TO CUH-LEANSE THIS CHILD - HEEEEALLL!!
AK!
HEY! STOP THAT!

TEK THAT YER BIG BASTARD!
STAND ASIDE, CHILD!
OooOOH!
- LEAVE HER ALONE!!
SHE'S POSESSED!
POSESSED? HMM - TIME TO CAST OUT SOME "MONEYCHANGERS" I THINK!...

STOP!

GRRRRRR! GRRRR!

...AND I BEHELD WHEN HE HAD OPENED THE SIXTH SEAL AND LO THERE WAS A GREAT EARTH-QUAKE; AND THE SUN BECAME BLACK AS SACKCLOTH OF HAIR AND THE MOON BECAME AS BLOOD!
MILK SHAKE FOAM

AND THE STARS OF HEAVEN FELL UNTO THE EARTH, EVEN AS THE FIG TREE CASTETH HER UNTIMELY FIGS WHEN SHE IS SHAKEN BY A MIGHTY WIND-
BELCH!!
RRED RRUUM! RRED RRUUM!!
GARLIC
AAAAARGH!!

PHEW! THERE NOW! -AND I NEVER LAID A FINGER ON THEM
wWAOWWW!
WELL COME ON THEN- LET'S GET GOING!

AT THE BUS STATION
THERE YOU ARE- -YOU LOOK HUMAN AGAIN, ANYWAY!
PHONE
THANKS

...THAT'S ALL FIXED UP -YOUR FOLKS ARE GOING TO MEET YOU AT THE OTHER END - HERE'S YOUR BUS TICKET - AND I GAVE CHRISTINA A PIECE OF MY MIND TOO!
OH GOOD! HANG ONTO IT A MOMENT -I SEE SOMEBODY OVER THERE I'M INDEBTED TO...

THANKS FOR THE LOAN OF YOUR THINGS... BYE!
Zzzz

sniff - THANKS, EVERYONE! I CAN'T REMEMBER WHEN I'VE BEEN TREATED SO KINDLY! sniff!
DON'T MENTION IT! -AND IF YOUR MA GIVES YOU ANY GRIEF, DO THAT 'EXORCIST' THING ON HER - IT SURE SCARED THE HELL OUT OF ME!...
STAND
GOODBYE! HAVE A SAFE JOURNEY
IN FACT, AH RECKON WE KNOW A SONG ABOUT THAT, DUN'T WE, GIRLS?..

SHE'S GOT A TICKET TO RII-IDE, AND SHE DON'T CARE!!
bye
Regional EXPRES

...DAMN! THAT TICKET COMPLETELY CLEANED US OUT- -ALL THAT BUSKING FOR NOTHING!
AH WELL...
YEAH...'EY- "AYE AAM THE ANT-EYE BUSKER, HERE'S TEN PEE", ANYWAY!
I SUPPOSE I COULD HAVE JUST WRITTEN 'RAG' A CHEQUE IN THE FIRST PLACE!...

Picnic

...or is it a takeaway? (featuring little red cagoul)

...OH GOD! ARE YOU ALL RIGHT ?!
WHUH? EH?
-WHAT ARE YOU DOING HERE? THIS IS THE PAINTBALL RANGE
IT IS?
-SO THAT'S WHAT THE TAPE WAS FOR!...
GREEN
D'YOU HAVE ANY PAIN? DIZZINESS? -I'M A MEDIC.
I DON'T THINK SO...
CAN YOU STAND?
"OOH MY CALF! OUCH! I THINK I'VE PULLED A MUSCLE!"
...WHICH LEG? MAYBE IF I SUPPORT THAT SIDE, YOU COULD WALK...
WELL, I RECKON YOU OUGHT TO CARRY ME, YOU BIG BULLY!
-SHOOTING DEFENCELESS PICNICKERS AND MESSING UP THEIR JUMPERS,
I DON'T KNOW!...
OH, GOD, SORRY. YEAH, WHATEVER YOU WANT...
PURPLE FOUR TO PURPLE CHIEF -OFF OFF OFF!
I'VE GOT A CIVVY HERE WITH A DODGY FETLOCK, AND I'M TAKING HER OFF RANGE FOR A CHECKUP -OVER...
SSHK
WONDER HOW LONG I CAN STRETCH THIS OUT?
-VA VA VOOM!

WELL, Christina?

I did it for *her*, of course.

She's of such an age when she might be turned from the path of righteousness by the distractions of this corrupt world. Western civilization is falling, of course. A culture falls because the decay is so slow no-one notices what is happening until it is too late. The modern world is grown Godless and decadent by gentle, deadly degrees. I *had* to make sure Theresa was not pulled down into a whirlpool of casual sins - I had to forge in her a sense of duty and obedience if she were to have the strength to resist temptation. My eyes have always been unduly sensitive to light, ever since childhood - *'Eyes no better, then?'* my relatives would say, each time I visited. I realised Theresa needed a task, a focus for discipline. I would ask her to read me some small print, say, or parts of our pocket Bible. Soon I was visiting the eye clinic more & more often, giving ever more sorrowful & incorrect answers to their eye tests. At last, they declared me legally blind, but I took pains to declare the affliction total to the family. Theresa was now bound to her duty; she should lead me, and read to me, and choose clothing and so on. Thus would I keep her by me, away from the garish lure of a rotting world, until she was of age to legally leave home, by which time I hoped to have persuaded her to take up holy orders and tend to the sick as she had tended to me.

(sigh) It was my own weakness which undid my plan.

A moment's indiscretion, reading a silly novel. Theresa must have seen me. The next day she was gone, run away to be with her addle-pated cousin and her pagan friend.

Oh, she returned by and by, covered in dirt and full of the *'ways of the world'*. She was utterly ruined. She's whipping up the family to have her move in with my brother, Heaven save her.

I don't regret what I tried to do.

I only curse the fact that I failed her.

Thai Dye! Sun. 8th T-19

...AND I SAID, SINEAD O'CONNOR'S ON AT THE RIVERSIDE THIS THURSDAY, AND HE SAID DID I WANT TO GO, SO WE'RE GOING! AND IF SHE DOES "TROY", I'LL JUST DROP DEAD ON THE SPOT WITH HAPPINESS!!

OOOUGHH!

SCRUB SCRUB

Speaking in Tongues   Wed. 11th T-16

1: HOW ARE YOU? 2: WHERE HAVE YOU BEEN? 3: WHERE DO YOU COME FROM? 4: WHAT?

27
Seconds
Thu. 12th T-15
4027
CLICK CLACK
CLICK CLACK
..."I'll break you, Sapphire, if it's the last thing I do" spat Rip, huskily...
Lace XII
SCREEEEEE
W-WAIT A MINUTE -
-THIS IS MY STOP!
27... AARGH!...25...24...
Lace XII
23...22...21...20...19...
STUFF!
SHOVE!
COLLATE!
FILE!
GRAB!

18...17...16...15...
SHOVE!
ZIP!
14...13...12... OOPS!
SQUELCH!
ZZZIP
ZZZZIP
10...9...8...7...6...5!...
PARP!
STAND CLEAR OF THE DOORS PLEASE!
4!..3!..2!..1!?...
FSSH!
FSSH!
ZERO! – PHEW, MADE IT!!
PTOO
RUMBLE
RUMBLE
RUMBLE
RUMBLE
OHH SUGAR!

Friday 13th... (down at the Chris-cave) T-14

...Scoring Points

...Part II or: the last temptation of Chris or: Late Night Double Feature Picture Show about midnight

SSSHHHHHHHHHHH
ZZZZZZ
FISSSSSHH...
Yawwwn...
...H'LO!...
...LOOKS LIKE I DID SLEEP WITH YOU AFTER ALL!
HUP... ...GO TURN SOME WINE INTO WATER...
SNORT
BRR! S'COLD!...
...SHAME THERE'S NO SHOWER...
...UGH! WHAT A SIGHT!...
FSSHHHHH
SSSSSHH
SSH
SLAP
SLAP
S'BETTER...
NOW... WHAT'S TO EAT?...
Super Loopz
SOMETHING UN-CHALLENGING...
MILK... EGGIES...
HONEY
BEETLE JUICE
...THOUGHT I HEARD YOU IN HERE - OH, FOOD! MMMMMM! "FOOD GOOOD!"
HI! - FOOD MAYBE GOOD, BUT DRINK BAAAD! - IT'S PANCAKES - CAN'T FACE ANY-THING HEAVY THIS MORNING
SHH! SHH!
MMMMM - CREATURE HUNGRY!
- CREATURE GO PUT COFFEE ON! IT'S NOT DONE YET!...
SSSSSSSS
THIS TOUCHING SCENE NOW AVAILABLE AS A TRADING CARD!
*23
C 447
IT'S NOT DONE YET!
COOKING
FIN!

Hair

Mon. 16th T-11

... YEAH, IT'S TAKEN A BIT OF ORGANISING - I HAD TO RING PETRA TO POST ME THE PROVISIONAL LICENSE I GOT LAST SUMMER, FROM WHEN I LAST HAD LESSONS
SHUSH! STOP MOVING ABOUT
HMM... LOSE THE SPLIT ENDS, & GIVE IT A NEW EDGE...
SORRY
-SO WHEN'S THIS HAPPENING, THEN?
WHRR
FRIDAY EVENING - HE'S ON HOSPITAL SHIFTS BEFORE THEN...
... I'M GOING TO CHECK IF HE'S IN ON WEDNESDAY MORNING, THOUGH - HE SAID HE MIGHT GET THAT OFF-
-OUCH!
SORRY! SHOULD OIL IT MORE OFTEN!
PEACH POMADE
RIGHT- NO TURNING BACK! YOU SURE?
SURE. GO AHEAD...
WHEE!
MAKE IT STRAIGHT UP THE BACK, COULD YOU?
OOH, BRUTAL!
AS YOU LIKE...
OH NO, JO! ALL YOUR LOVELY HAIR!
THERE Y'GO - NOT BAD.
DON'T GET IN A PANIC!
- I DO THIS EVERY YEAR, SO IT'S COOLER FOR SUMMER
- BUT ANYWAY, WAIT 'TIL CHRIS SEES IT - HE'LL BE BOWLED OVER!
I DON'T KNOW - CHRIS THIS, CHRIS THAT - - WHAT WAS THAT QUOTE AGAIN: "ABOVE ALL ELSE, TO THINE OWN SELF BE TRUE?"
THAT'S A BIT RICH, COMING FROM THE GIRL WHO'S HAD ABOUT FIFTY 'IMAGES' IN THE LAST SIX MONTHS!
HMM! TOUCHÉ!
..JUST A BIT OF SHAPING AND WE'RE DONE..
RIGHT, THEN! SEE YOU NEXT YEAR!
THANKS!
C'MON, PANDA - LET'S GO STUN THE PUBLIC!
COR!
TA VERY MUCH!
KEEP THE CHANGE
OOH I FEEL PRITEE OH SO PRITEE ... YUM TUM DUM DUM DEDUM DUM DE DOOO!...
ching
- ARE YOU COMING, OR WHAT?
OH, JO...

Who's That Girl? Wed. 18th T-9

Whuh? EH? WHO ARE YOU?
WHO AM I? - WHO ARE YOU, IN, IN CHRIS'S BED, YOU, YOU...
JO! I DIDN'T HEAR YOU COME IN!
CHRIS! HOW COULD YOU, YOU DIRTY TWOTIMING...
EH? BUH - JO! JO! THIS IS RUTH - MY TWIN SISTER!
SHE - WHUH - SISTER?
- SHE'S UP HERE UNEXPECTED, I LET HER HAVE THE BED AND I CRASHED ON THE SOFA!
ohhh GHOOD what a BALLOON!..
i am SO sorry
(yawn) uh, DOESN'T MATTER... EASY MISTAKE TO MAKE. - YOU'RE JO, RIGHT?
YEAH. RUTH. er, HELLO, RUTH! sorry!
...RUTH'S UP HERE MODELLING FOR A WEEK OR SO - - SHE MODELS, YOU KNOW.
HMM... NOW THAT YOU MENTION IT...
...HAVE I SEEN YOU SOMEWHERE BEFORE, RUTH?
HMM... IT WAS PROBABLY THAT CHOCOLATE BAR ADVERT ON TELLY THAT I DID.
OOH, YES! YOU'RE THE ONE PACKING A CASE AND EATING AN "OVATION" BAR!
(sigh) YUP, THAT'S ME!..
HEY, IF YOU DO ADVERTS, THEN, I DON'T SUPPOSE YOU KNOW VERITY BOURNEVILLE AT ALL?
WHO, 'CHOCCY VERY'? OF COURSE I DO! - - SAME AGENT.
WOW!
- WE WERE AT TYCHO SCHOOL TOGETHER! SHE WAS MY BEST FRIEND!
?!
WHAT? - YOU AND VERY WENT TO TYCHO?
UH HUH
- BUT I WENT TO TYCHO TOO!!

SCREEEAM!!
WHAT FORM WERE YOU? - I NEVER SAW YOU
"KEPLER" THIRD -
- ME NEITHER
"ADAM WHITE-HEAD" HOUSE-
- WE MUST HAVE JUST MISSED EACH OTHER.
HEY - RIGHT... "TYCHO, TYCHO BRA-HE"...
"HAD A GOLDEN NOSE!!"
"...LOST IT IN A SWORD FIGHT, OR SO THE STORY GOES..."
"...WATCHED THE SKIES IN DEN-MARK WITHOUT A TEL-E-SCOPE..."
"...HE KEPT A DWARF AND PARTIED HARD AND WENT TO SERVE THE POPE!"
hee hee hee hee hee hee!
DUHHH... THIS IS OBVIOUSLY SOME SORT OF WEIRD DREAM... I'LL WAKE UP FOR REAL IN A MO!..
Interlude: Girls On Film
the next day
AH COULD MURDER A PINT
GAGGIN' MATE!
SPITTIN' FEWERS!
OKAY LOVEY BIG SMILE THAAT'S IT, SLINKY, LOVEY, HEAD BACK GOOD DEAR, NOW SWEEP Y'HAIR...
KZZZIT KZZZIT KZZZIT
pop
- I RECKON THIS NEEDS A BRUNETTE! - FANCY A GO, JO?
ERM! - NO, BUT I KNOW A GIRL WHO WOULD...
- DAMN! SHOULD HAVE ASKED PANDA ALONG!...
SHE'S LOOKING GOOD
NICE HALL, GOOD ACOUSTIC

What is Dadah / The Empress's New Clothes Thu. 19th T-8

"HELL DRIVERS"
Fri 20th
T-7
DAMN! THOSE BEASTIE BOY FANS HAVE NICKED MY BADGE!...
ARE YOU SURE YOU WANT TO COME? IT'LL BE JUST A LOT OF DULL REVERSING AND PARKING AND STUFF.
OH NO, I THINK IT'LL BE FUN- AND I CAN TEST YOU ON THE BOOK OF HIGHWAY CODES, TOO...
OKAY, JO, JUST START HER UP AND LET'S SEE WHAT YOU KNOW ALREADY.
BRM!
-START HIM UP, YOU MEAN! ALL CARS ARE 'HIMS', DIDN'T YOU KNOW?
SCREEE
WHOOPS! LUCKY THERE WASN'T ANYTHING IN FRONT!
WHEW! WELL, YOU'RE CERTAINLY PAST THE "BUNNY HOPS" STAGE!
YEAH, YEAH! EASY PEASY...
GB
FOW 242W
...HOWSABOUT THAT NEW MOTORWAY, CHRIS? -I NEVER DID GET UP TO DOING MOTORWAYS
ERR... I'M NOT SURE IF IT'S ENTIRELY LEGAL FOR LEARNERS...
BRUMM
M69
SCREEEEEEEE
FOW 242W
er, SANDY, COULD YOU PASS ME THE HIGHWAY CODE?
SANDRA.
AH- I WAS RIGHT- YOUR LICENSE ONLY GOES UP TO A-ROADS
TOO LATE- WE'RE ON IT! -MIGHT AS WELL TRY IT OUT, EH? WE'VE NO L-PLATES ON ANYWAY, SO NO-ONE'LL KNOW!
GB
FOW 242W
OH, BUGGER! I FORGOT ABOUT THAT- -WE'RE REALLY PUSHING IT NOW!!
WH- ARE YOU BREAKING THE LAW, JO?

OH, DON'T BE SUCH A PAIR OF OLD WOMEN! WE WON'T NEED LONG ON HERE TO LEARN THE ROPES- -I MEAN, LOOK- THERE'S NOTHING TO HIT, IS THERE?
OH, YOU'D BE SURPRISED!..

JO!- YOU OVERTAKE ON THE OTHER SIDE! YOU'RE GOING TO GET US BOTH NICKED!!
WHOOPS! IMPORTANT SAFETY TIP! I'LL BEAR IT IN MIND...
UBU

THERE, NOW, SATISFIED? -NICE STRAIGHT LINE.
...AREN'T WE GOING A BIT FAST?
RATHER! JO! ARE YOU TRYING TO COLLECT THE SET OR SOMETHING? THE LIMIT'S 70, NOT...NINETY-THREE?

LOOK, I KNOW WHAT I'M DOING, I KNOW WE'RE NOT GOING TO CRASH OR ANYTHING
WATCH THE ROAD!
YOU'RE SO SURE?!

...YEAH, MY MA AND ME WENT TO A FORTUNE TELLER ONCE, AND SHE SAID THAT I WOULD LIVE TO BE REALLY OLD AND TRAVEL A LONG WAY- WELL, NOTHING CAN HAPPEN, CAN IT?? I HAVEN'T BEEN ANYWHERE YET!!
WILL YOU WATCH THE BASTARD ROAD, JO!?!

GHOOOOD!
-AW, CHRIS, I NEVER THOUGHT YOU'D TURN WIMPY!
HEY! EVEN IF WHAT YOU SAY IS TRUE, YOU MIGHT NOT BE HURT, BUT THAT DOESN'T COVER US, DOES IT??

NNNGGH... I SUPPOSE SO... -I'D BETTER TAKE THE NEXT TURNOFF BEFORE YOU TWO BABIES DIE OF FRIGHT, THEN!...
I SHOULD THINK SO TOO!

...OH, CHRIIISSS... -I FORGOT TO MENTION, I NEVER DID QUITE GET THE HANG OF PARKING...THAT SHOULD BE SOME FUN ALL RIGHT!...
ohhh NOOO!...
FOW 242W
STOP

All too much (for me to take) Wed. 25th T-2

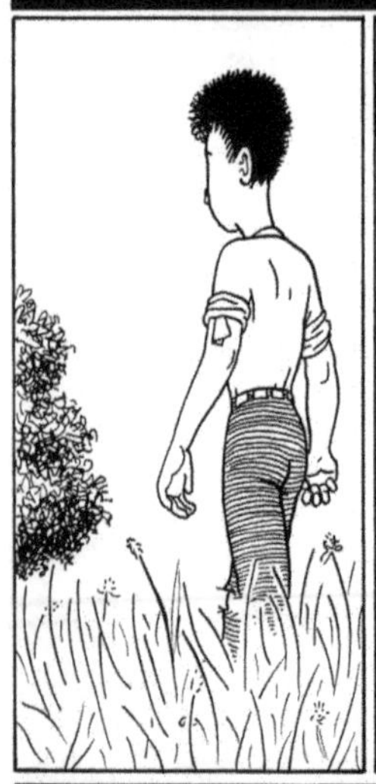

WHAT A BASKET CASE!
I'M SORRY FOR IGNORING YOU. WHY DIDN'T YOU JUST TELL ME BEFORE? YOU'VE BOTTLED IT ALL UP AGAIN, LIKE AT CHRISTMAS, HAVEN'T YOU?
=huck= yes you're right i have...
LOOK, I'M BUSY TOMORROW, BUT WHY DON'T WE HAVE THE WHOLE OF FRIDAY? - GO TO THE SEASIDE OR SOMETHING.
yes i'd love that
...YOU HAVE TO TELL ME ONE THING FIRST, THOUGH...
WHAT'S THAT?
HOW THE HELL DO I GET DOWN?!
This Sporting Life
Thu. 26th T-1
...THE EYEBROWS? AH. YES, IT'S BLEACHED - I DO IT TO MATCH MY LITTLE BROTHER OVER THERE - WE'RE A "PIGEON PAIR", NOT EVEN SLIGHTLY I.D.
LITTLE?
GRR
GRUNT
UGH
OOF
GNASH
...WELL, I AM TWENTY MINUTES OLDER THAN HIM... (sigh) I GET THE LOOKS AND HE GETS THE INSANE URGE TO ROLL AROUND IN THE MUD!
YEAH... GOD, RUTH, WHY DID IT HAVE TO BE RUGBY?..
...I BLOODY HATE RUGBY, IT'S JUST A BIG PUB FIGHT WITH A BALL INSTEAD OF A PUB!
YEAH
RIGHT!
WHAT'VE YOU LOAD OF FATTIES, SKIVERS AND WEIRDOS COME UP WITH FOR AN EXCUSE THIS TIME?
-OOH, INCREDIBLY NASTY PERIODS!
-I'M PSYCHOLOGICALLY DISTURBED
er, cough! cough!?
...MUST DO IT TO WORK OFF ALL THAT CAVEMAN "HUNT FIGHT KILL" STUFF I SUPPOSE...
HMM...
-HEY, IS HE COMING THIS WAY?..
SPLUDGE
-DID YOU SEE THAT TACKLE?!...

ON THE BEACH Fri. 27th Today

HEY - I'VE GOT TO GET A PICTURE OF THIS - - GIVE US A POSE!
HOW'S THIS?
CLIK! WHIZZ
- NOW I WANT TO DO A PICTURE OF YOU TO TAKE HOME!...

OKAY...
YOU LOOK THROUGH THERE, AND YOU PRESS THAT...
OH PISH TUSH! I KNOW!
- WHO BOUGHT YOU IT IN THE FIRST PLACE?
CLIK! WHIZZ

MMM... THIS REMINDS ME OF WHEN WE USED TO VISIT AUNTY ANNA IN SWANAGE... ME AND PETRA WOULD PADDLE, AND BUILD SANDCASTLES WITH THE TWINS AND STUFF... MMM
PADDLE? IN A BOAT OR SOMETHING?

NO, NO - IT MEANS, SORT OF, WALKING ABOUT IN THE WAVES, WHEN YOU CAN'T BE BOTHERED TO SWIM - - "PLODGING" THEY CALL IT, ROUND HERE.
"PLODGE"! I LIKE THAT! SHALL WE PLODGE? hee hee
YEAH! - IF YOU LIKE...

YOU'RE RIGHT ABOUT THIS WEATHER - I THINK I'LL STAY BAREFOOT - - ON THE BEACH, ANYWAY!
COME ON THEN!
OKAY...

HERE I GO!...
EEURRRGGGHH!!
THE SEA'S COLD! - HOW IS IT COLD?!
- YOU'RE A LONG WAY FROM THE INDIAN OCEAN NOW, DEAR!

...OH NO, NO WAY! - I'D NEVER HAVE TRIED IF I'D KNOWN IT WAS COLD!...
CHUH! WHAT A WIMP!...

IT'S O.K. - THE 'MAIDEN' CAN PLAY IF PARTNERED BY THE TWINS...
- NOW NOW! BAT HARDER OR PLAY WITHOUT SHOES!...
"HANGMAN'S CRICKET"? - THIS GAME HAS EVERYTHING IN IT BUT THE KITCHEN SINK!...
...WELL, YOU DIG HOLES WITH THAT, AND CATCH CRABS IN THAT, AND FILL THAT UP WITH SAND TO MAKE SANDCASTLES
AH - LIKE A MOULD - CLEVER! BUT IN MY CASE, OF COURSE THEY'D BE... SANDRA-CASTLES!?
GROAN!
20
Beach

WHUPS! WATCH OUT!..
OH! SORRY!
THUMP!

...CAN WE HAVE OUR BALL BACK, MISTER?
LBW!
WHA? CERTAINLY...

...AND THAT'S MISS, ACTUALLY!!...
giggle!

...BLOODY NERVE! GOD, MY HAIR'S SHORT, BUT-'MISTER'!?!?...
WELL, I THINK IT MAKES YOU LOOK... ...WHAT'S THE WORD... ...HANDSOME?
'BUTCH' PERHAPS?
NOPE - -SORRY, CHRIS, BUT I'M GROWING IT OUT AGAIN!...

...SHALL WE STOP HERE FOR A BIT? I FEEL LIKE SOAKING UP SOME SUN.
OKAY - I CAN HAVE A LOOK AT SOME MORE THINGS I'VE BOUGHT...

HEY! IS THAT A TINY TELLY IN THERE? COR!
EH? OH- THAT'S NOT-

YOU DIDN'T SAY YOU HAD ONE OF THESE! HOW D'YOU WORK IT?
AH! ER, UNFORTUNATELY, IT'S A SPECIAL ONE- -IT ONLY PICKS UP THAI T.V.!...
OH. NEVER MIND!..

MMMMMMMMMMMM!...
RIGHT, LET'S HAVE A LOOK AT THIS - ...OOH, LOTS OF PICTURES!...
BIG KIDS BOOK OF FACTS

AWWW
WHAT?
- IT SAYS IN HERE THAT GIANT GROUND SLOTHS ARE EXTINCT.
'FRAID SO...
- HEY, DID YOU KNOW THAT TUMULOKS ARE EXTINCT TOO?
HUH?...
BIG KIDS BOOK OF

AH NOW, WHERE TO BEGIN? SHE WAS MY BEST FRIEND - QUITE POTTY, VERY WORLDLY. SHE CAME UP WITH THE MOST STUPEFYING EXCUSES AND LIES I'VE EVER HEARD - FOR INSTANCE...

BOURNEVILLE! DRIBBLE! YA LATE!

AH, WELL, MISS, YOU SEE, WE WERE WALKING TO CLASS, AND ALL OF A SUDDEN, JO CAUGHT LEPROSY AND HER NOSE FELL OFF AND WE HAD TO STOP AND LOOK FOR IT. IT'S GOT BETTER, THOUGH, AS YOU CAN SEE, SO WE DON'T NEED TO GET HER A GOLD ONE LIKE TYCHO!...

SHE WAS COQUETTISH AS HELL, TOO... ...WE HAD THESE SCHOOL TRIPS TO THE SWIMMING BATHS - OUR SCHOOL HAD IT'S OWN ATOM SMASHER BUT NO POOL - AND THE NEARBY PUBLIC BOY'S SCHOOL SOMETIMES HAD THEM ALSO...

SHE HAD THIS BACKLESS ONE-PIECE BATHING SUIT, AND SHE WOULD STAND ON THE EDGE OF THE POOL WEARING IT, WAITING FOR SOME BOYS TO LOOK HER WAY...

-THEN SHE WOULD DO A BACK FLIP INTO THE WATER WITH HER ARMS OUT IN FRONT LIKE THIS...

THE TRICK IS, THE WATER GETS INTO THE SIDES OF THE SWIMSUIT AND SWEEPS IT OFF ALONG THE OUT-STRETCHED ARMS, SEE?

SO SHE WOULD CALMLY SWIM TO THE STEPS AND CLIMB OUT TOPLESS, HITCHING HERSELF BACK UP AS SHE WENT! - THE BOYS WERE GOB-SMACKED!

...AND THEN SHE'D DO IT AGAIN! EVENTUALLY MISS BUNTER WOULD NOTICE AND SEND VERITY BACK TO THE CHANGING ROOMS, BUT BY THEN, THE BOYS WERE PRACTICALLY VOMITING WITH LUST AND CLUTCHING THEIR SWIMMING TRUNKS - IT WAS HILARIOUS!!...

AHH-huh...
...sigh...

...WHAT'S THAT FOR?
"A PENNY FOR YOUR THOUGHTS" - I BELIEVE THAT'S THE CORRECT PHRASE?
OH. RIGHT. NO..., IT'S JUST... THINKING ABOUT THE BOYS GETTING WORKED UP JUST NOW, er...

mmm-HMM?
WELL, I REMEMBERED... ...YOU KNOW... ...ONE FRIDAY, CHRIS, ahh... ...'WANTED TO'
UMM?

BUUUT, I DIDN'T 'WANT TO'...
...WEELL, THE NEXT WEDNESDAY, I, er, DID 'WANT TO'... BUT WE COULDN'T, REALLY, BECAUSE HIS SISTER RUTH WAS THERE...
MM.
...BUT RUTH WENT HOME LAST NIGHT, SO WE COULD HAVE ... BUT...
...BUT NOW... I DON'T 'WANT TO' AGAIN...
..isn't that odd...

-WHUFF
-HEY! DID YOU KNOW RUTH BLEACHES HER HAIR? THERE'S SOMETHING YOU'VE NEVER TRIED - DIFFERENT COLOURS!...
sigh - WHY, THAT'S AN EXCELLENT IDEA! I RECKON I'LL DO JUST THAT SOON AS I GET HOME!...

LATER
HMM... ...I CAN HEAR FAR-OFF MUSIC...
YES... I THINK IT'S THAT FUNNY WOMAN OVER THERE, PLAYING HER PIANO...

..."SOMETIMES A THOUSAND TWANGLING INSTRUMENTS WILL HUM ABOUT MINE EARS; AND SOMETIMES VOICES, THAT, IF I THEN HAD WAKED AFTER A LONG SLEEP, WILL MAKE ME SLEEP AGAIN; AND THEN, IN DREAMING, THE CLOUDS, METHOUGHT, WOULD OPEN AND SHOW RICHES READY TO DROP UPON ME: THAT, WHEN I WAKED, I CRIED TO DREAM AGAIN".

OHHH, LOVELY- -DON'T TELL ME- -"THE TEMPEST" RIGHT?
-YEAH, WELL SPOTTED!...
IT SEEMS LIKE I'VE BEEN REHEARSING THAT ONE ALL MY LIFE — -I'LL HAVE TO LOBBY THE DRAMA SOC. TO DO IT NEXT TERM AS THEIR SHAKESPEARE "OFFERING"...

WHAT WAS IT AGAIN...
"FULL FATHOM FIVE THY FATHER LIES; OF HIS BONES ARE CORAL MADE; THOSE ARE PEARLS THAT WERE HIS EYES: NOTHING OF HIM THAT DOES FADE BUT DOES SUFFER A SEA CHANGE INTO SOMETHING RICH AND STRANGE."
HMMMM. I SUPPOSE HE DOES, REALLY.

at the station T-58 minutes

sigh
SENSIBLE AS ALWAYS!
-OKAY THEN! HELP ME LUG THE STUFF OVER TO PLATFORM 3 AND I'LL TEACH YOU SOMETHING ELSE!...
THUN TREN STANG PONG PAFOM TEE ZA SISTY TUTTY TOO FOW BUNGUM, KONG A DERM, DONGT'IN, YOK, DONKSA...
PHEW! THAT'S IT... -RIGHT! PAY ATTENTION- THIS IS HOW YOU SAY BYE TO AN ITALIAN...
SHEPPY, CHESSLE, DOBBY, BUNTON TENT, TAMF ANG BUM NOO SEAT...
SLAM
SLAM
THERE! ALL DONE! TIME TO GO!...
'BYE, PANDA! SEE YOU IN A MONTH! DON'T WORRY SO! ...BYE!
GOODBYE, JO.
BYE! SEE YA! TA RA!
...bye
3
...ARRAWAYWIYE HYEM CHER BUG HOOSE ANTAKYA MINGIN' MOLEEDS WI'YE!!
WHAT?
NAW FENCE HEN-JUSSA BUTTY BATHHOOSE Y'NAW
back at halls
T-16 minutes
THIS SHOULD COME IN VERY HANDY... I HOPE THEY DON'T MISS IT!...
UGH... WHERE TO BEGIN? ...ONLY GOT 15 MINUTES UNTIL 5:23 - THE "APPOINTED HOUR"...
...WISH JO COULD COME WITH ME... ...DON'T KNOW WHAT SHE'D MAKE OF IT ALL, THOUGH!...
HAY!

ohhh, NOT NOW!!...
PANDA...
UH HUH?
...I WAS JUST WONDERING...
...WHAT YOU WOULD SAY IF I SAID YOU WERE... "KON TAI KORNG BPLORM"?

er, NOT A LOT...
THAT IS STRANGE - IT MEANS "NOT A REAL THAI!"

YOU-
-OH, EXCUSE ME, I HAVE TO GO TO THE PORTER AND HAND IN MY KEYS!!...

HAY! COME BACK! YOU HAVE MUCH EXPLAINING TO DO!
'LEK'- I WAS JUST WONDERING WHAT YOU WOULD SAY IF I TOLD YOU TO SOD OFF!

LOOK, JUST LEAVE ME ALONE - THIS IS NONE OF YOUR BUSINESS!
-WHY DO YOU PRETEND TO BE THAI? WHAT ARE YOU HIDING?
WHO'S A GRUMPY SAUSAGE TODAY?
SCRAWL
CHING

MEANWHILE - 'UNAVOIDABLY DELAYED'...
...BLOODY HELL!
-DAM' SIGNALLING FAULT!...
THE
Alliance push Labour from second place
DRUM DRUM

...GONE TWENTY PAST FIVE, AND THE SODDING TRAIN'S ONLY TRAVELLED A FEW HUNDRED YARDS!
HARUMPH!!...
PARP! PAARRP!

LURCH!
UGH! OH WELL... HERE WE GO!...

HAY! HAY!
WHAT ARE YOU DOING? THAT IS JO'S ROOM! THIEF!
C'MON, C'MON! -JUST A FEW MOMENTS...
FUMBLE

-DON'T THINK YOU CAN HIDE IN THERE! COME OUT OR I WILL FETCH SOMEONE TO COME AND GET YOU OUT!...
SLAM
YOU DO THAT!
OPEN THIS DOOR! WHAT ARE YOU DOING IN THERE?
OOF!!!
WHOOF! MADE IT!...
TRIP!!!
¡Aiiii! ¡MIERDA!
OOF!
¡MERCEDES! ¡MUCHACHARONITA! ¿QUÉ TAL CONTIGO?
¡!
¡DOÑA! ¿QUE HACE USTED? -MIR'AL DESORDEN!

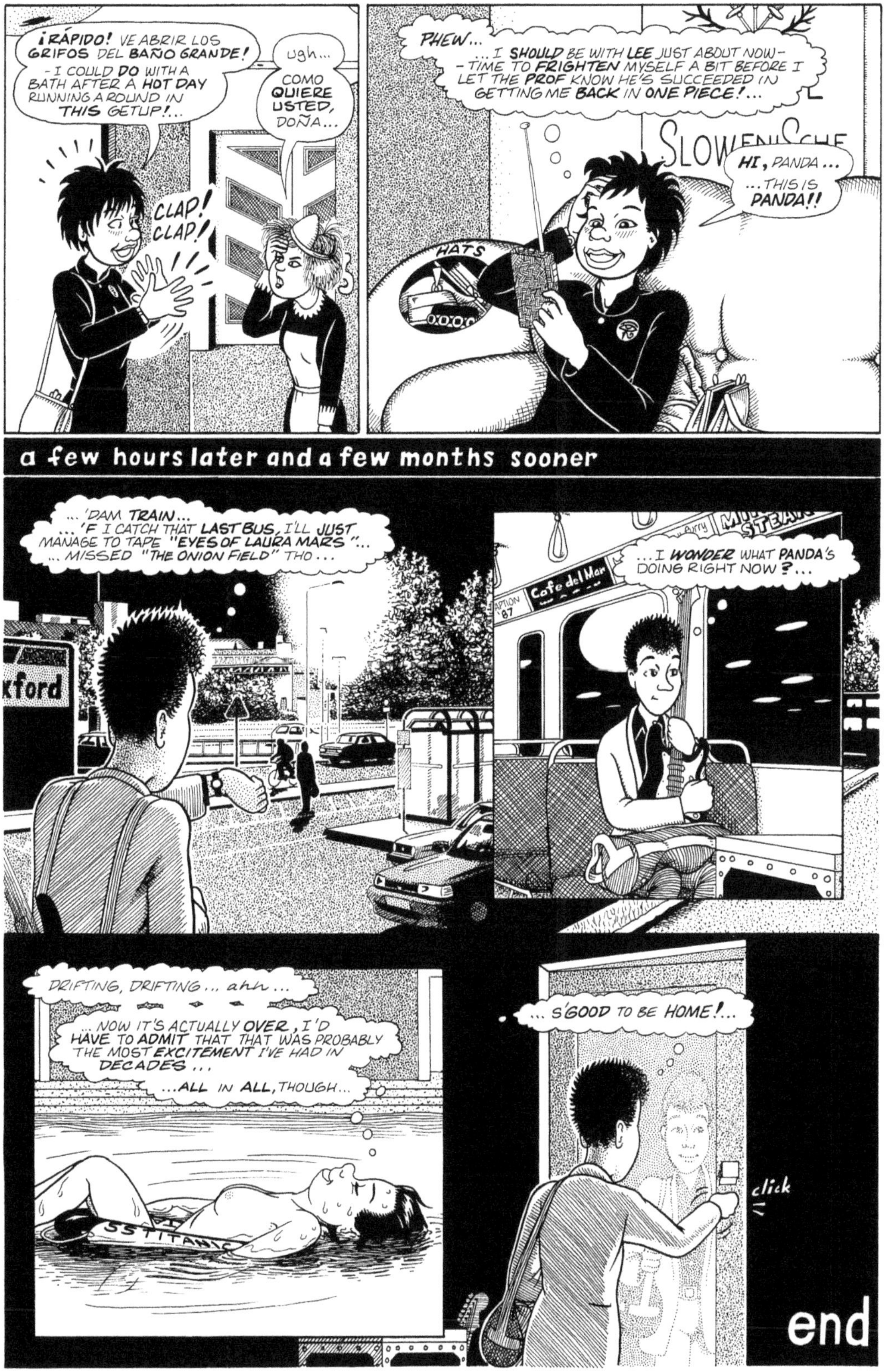

a few hours later and a few months sooner

...'DAM TRAIN... ...'F I CATCH THAT LAST BUS, I'LL JUST MANAGE TO TAPE "EYES OF LAURA MARS"... ...MISSED "THE ONION FIELD" THO...

xford

...I WONDER WHAT PANDA'S DOING RIGHT NOW?...

Cafe del Mar

DRIFTING, DRIFTING... ahh...

...NOW IT'S ACTUALLY OVER, I'D HAVE TO ADMIT THAT THAT WAS PROBABLY THE MOST EXCITEMENT I'VE HAD IN DECADES...

...ALL IN ALL, THOUGH...

SSTITANIC

...S'GOOD TO BE HOME!...

click

end

After Words

Concern Grows For Missing Girl Student

Mystery surrounds the disappearance of Novocastria University student Sandra Castle who has been missing since the end of last term.

Sandra (19) - an overseas student from Thailand and known as 'Panda' to her small circle of friends - was last seen around the corridors of Ethel Merman Hall on the last day of term by fellow Thai student Aporanee Petbun who said that she had been acting strangely for some time.

Miss Petbun said "I met her for the first time only a few weeks ago. From the first I knew she was wrong - she always avoided me and did not seem to speak Thai.

Jocasta Dribble - Miss Castle's neighbour and closest friend - had said goodbye to her only a short while before when she left for home for the Easter break; "She saw me off at the station. She didn't say anything about going away for the vacation"

The Police are looking into the disappearance.

Missing: Sandra Carter ??

Dismantled Pope

Possible Drugs Link Over Missing Student

A dramatic twist has occurred in the investigation into the case of missing girl student Sandra 'Panda' Carter who vanished on the last day of term at the University.

After interviewing her friends the Police have discovered that she often talked about her father being involved in Thailand's notorious drugs trade - although the seems to be some doubt as to her real nationality.

One friend - Jocasta Dribble - said "she was always throwing money around, especially on clothes and stuff. The first time I asked her where she got it from she said that her dad was a drug smuggler back home, but you could never tell if she was being serious".

Clothes

All her belongings were left in her room at Ethel Merman Hall, although a number of her clothes are missing. Adding further doubt to her nationality is the manner in which she had decorated her room; what her friends had thought were Thai ornaments have turned out to have been bought in a local Chinese supermarket.

EnJoy 23/5

Mystery Grows Over Thai Girl

Missing Thai student Sandra Castle (19) continues to remain a puzzle to the Police and her friends.

Ongoing investigations have revealed a number of mysteries about the girl, including the fact that she did not seem to actually be a student at the University - despite living in University accommodation and passing herself off as one.

No academic records exist for her and paperwork in the housing office has turned out to be forgeries. Her given home address in Thailand does not exist.

No-one from the University was available for comment.

...ooks just like a real rabbit but isn... one.

Missing Girl

Police have announced that the investigation inot the disappearance of University student Sandra Castle has been put "on hold", although the case will remain open "for the forseeable future".

Calendar Girl

APRIL

DISAPPEARED? NO, THERE'S BEEN A MISTAKE, SURELY... I MEAN, SHE'S OBVIOUSLY JUST GONE HOME... ...I MEAN, WHY WOULD SHE LEAVE ALL THAT STUFF BEHIND IF SHE WASN'T... LOOK, JUST QUIT WINDING ME UP, RIGHT, I DON'T WANT TO HEAR ANY MORE...

MAY

JUNE

JULY

AUGUST

SEPTEMBER

OCTOBER

NOVEMBER

DECEMBER

OH, THIS IS IDIOTIC!...

JANUARY 1988

FEBRUARY

MARCH...

and finally...

THREE 'LOST TALES'

The idea for this came from a sketch in a letter.

When we were preparing **Good Morning Vietgrove**, I sent letters with rough sheets to most of the Women Cartoonists featured within, just in case they had any objections. When the reply came back from Jeremy Dennis, she'd added little sketches of Jo and Panda to her letter. This was a strange feeling for me, since I'd never seen these two drawn by anybody else but me. Here they were, and I never drew them! They were free of me!

It got me thinking about maybe having *extra* stories, drawn by guest artists, in the back of **Director's Cut #0.** Whenever I draw the characters, what you see is my attempt to represent the *ideal* Jo or Panda - if someone else drew them, would you get the same *ideal* showing through the different styles? Or am I talking rubbish?

Let's find out... ***T.W.***

It must, indeed be strange for Terry to see these stories - he having no input into them. It's certainly weird for me; Jeremy's story has no contribution from either of us, Lee K's was 100% written by me and I've not seen a Jo and Panda story of mine done by anyone other than Terry, and Lee B-W's is *loosely* based on an outline of mine (and completed in a last-minute marathon effort - 4 pages in 1½ days) and all certainly offer a different change of pace and style.

Is this an experiment we should repeat? ***D.McK.***

Lee Kennedy's the woman behind **Wage Slave, Little Girl Blues**, and **Inner City Pagan.** She's also seen fame in **Monkey Punk, Fanny, Ground Level, Blat!, Automatic, The Girly Comic** etc. plus illos for at least two books. She lives in South London with a crazy cat called Amazy, and a delicate constitution.

Contact: Lee Kennedy, 58 Durrington Tower, Westbury, Wandsworth Road, London SW8 3LF Email: sheelanagig69@hotmail.com

Lee Brimmicombe-Wood is the wild-eyed Brush Monster behind **Echidna Variations** and **Toms,** plus many articles and reviews for magazines (**Arcane, Manga Mania** etc.), one or two books (**ALIENS Colonial Marines Technical Manual**) and many, many board & console games.

If you step within eight feet of him, he will make you tea and show you more Anime and Manga than the human frame can stand, until you go *"Bwaa-haa-haaa!"*

Email: lee@damfine.demon.co.uk

Jeremy Dennis is a woman, in case you didn't know. She's been involved in several dozen minicomics from A4 down to postage-stamp size, including **3 in a Bed, Minute Steaks, Jessamy & the Bird, Alien8,** plus hundreds of entries on her Weekly Strip blog AND had time to be published in **GirlFrenzy** and **Fanny**, AND to get married and become **Jeremy Day.**

Her hobbies include drawing, dinosaurs, kittens and electro-pop music.

Email: jrd@jeremydennis.co.uk blog: jeremyday.org.uk

The Rules of the Game PART ONE
... In which Panda becomes much confused ...
What's it to be, then?
COCKROACH BAR. 8:43pm
..erm, Grand Marnier and soda, please
WHAAAAAA-
That's what I WANT, OK?
JO-JO! over here!
? ... Someone's shouting for you.
I suppose so-
It's Steve and his crowd- Shall we say Hi?
...er... Curtis Auditorium
obvious-
SCAN office!
ohhh- dodgy!

Hi, Jo, Sandra take a pew. You know everyone, don't you?
Erm..?
Claremont Bridge!
What's going on?
OOCH!
Main Library!
Kensington Terrace - like Mornington Crescent, natch!
Hey, are you going to take your turn or what?
Ah, this is great this..
Yeah! It's an ancient game based on places in London - only we play it with university locations... We've just had SCAN office to Claremont Bridge. That's a bit like Edirlop to Vauxhall Bridge. then there was...
Oh?
Old or new?
Dammit - NEW
Right, Robinson Library St. Thomas the Communist!
...a slide right to the Robinson Library (allowed because it's just been built - like Lloyds) and Steve's just Reverse-Looped into St. Thomas' Church, putting Charly there in Nip!...
You're not serious?
Oh! Nicely done! He's side-slipped Steve's Nip and opened up the game to Quartering - a bit like using the Park Lane shortcut...
Wha-?
Charly says "Theatre Carpark"

Richardson Road...
KENSINGTON TERRACE!
Woo!
CLAP CLAP
CLAP
Bravo!
CLAP
CLAP
Yep! Obvious, really! Mind you, under Finche's Rules, that wouldn't have been allowed...
CLAP
CLAP
Yes, but NOBODY's played Finche's Rules for years...
NO-ONE WHO TAKES THE GAME SERIOUSLY!
Hee hee
Ha Ha
Yuk yuk
I'll get my coat...
LEE KENNEDY 4.96

THE RULES OF THE GAME part II

HERE'S THE REST OF THE CROWD -- ALEX, NICK AND MATT, OUR D.M. GRAB A PEW!
??
HI! IT'S GOOD TO SEE MORE FEMALES JOINING IN!
YOU PLAYED BEFORE, PANDA?
YOU HAVE TO BE MAD TO PLAY WITH US!
DRAGONSTUFF

GWAN! BUDGE UP ON THE BED!
WE'VE GOT SOME SPARE CHARACTERS FOR YOU TO PLAY, PANDA!

YEAH, WE GOT NICK'S ELF, FARANGORN; WE GOT A FIGHTER/MAGE, WE --
-- UH, WOULD YOU PREFER TO PLAY A LAWFUL OR CHAOTIC CHARACTER?

JUSTINE? EXACTLY HOW DO YOU PLAY THIS GAME?

THINK OF IT AS A GAME OF *MAKE BELIEVE!*
?!

LATER.
SWSSH!
TK!
THHK!
UFFF!?
HNNNH!
ERK!
SHINK!

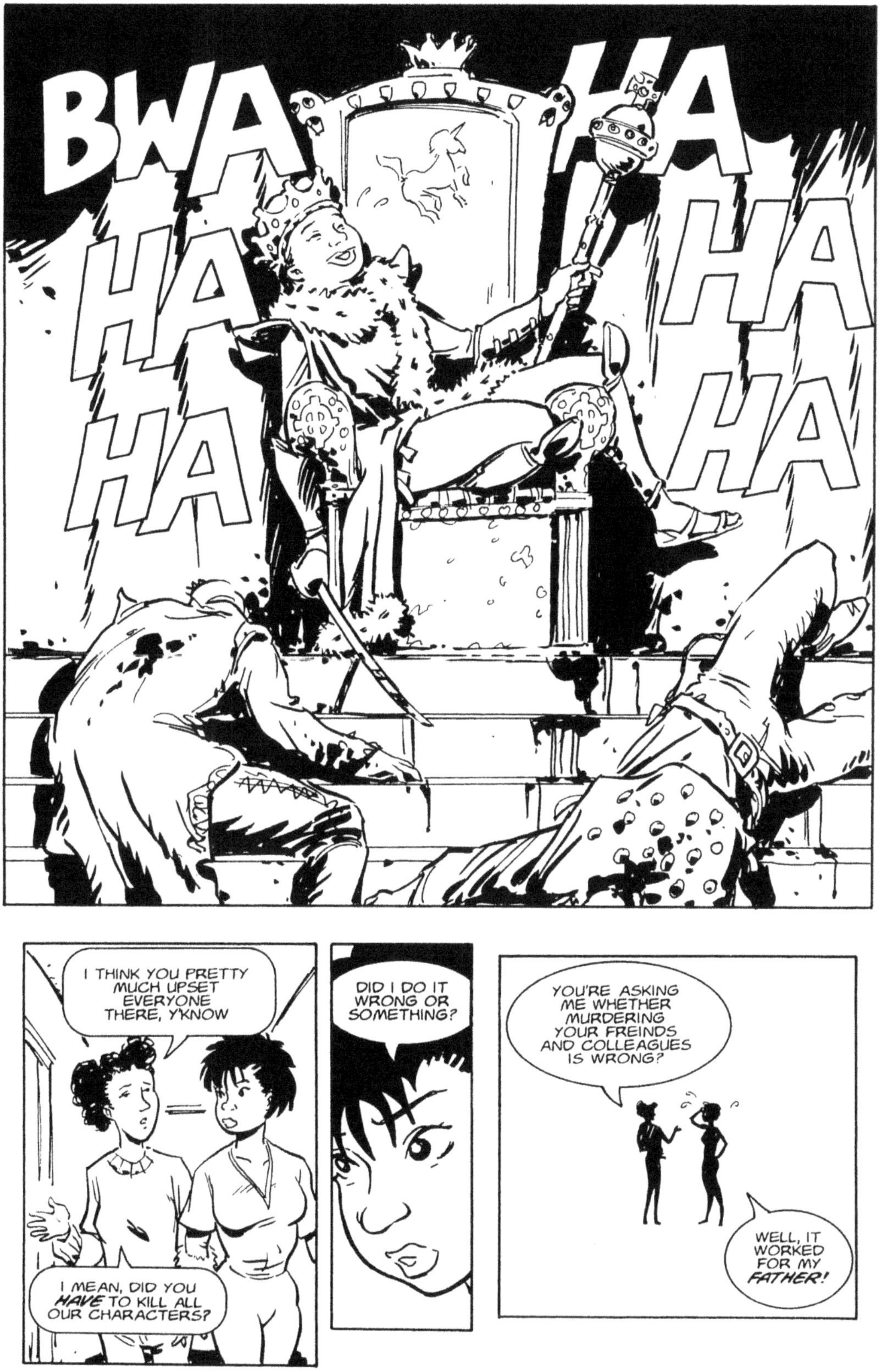

BWA HA HA HA HA HA HA HA HA

We've been to button moon
We've followed Mr Spoon
BUTTON MOON!
LIFE BEFORE PINGU
ROMPI ROM RO RO ROM
Tsk.
Back to work-(sigh)
yawn
Let's see... it's kid's TV this week - so no more "research" for HOURS
work work work...
I wonder if there's an essay I can set them which will make it impossible for them to write about The Magic Roundabout?
still... it IS a classic... hmm. Penguin classics... penguins, penguins... penguins in children's television?
auk auk auk
hum hum oo.
are there any penguins in childrens TV?
ham-hum. So - "Identifying with the animal in educational television?"
squeak
slump
I'm sure I've read that essay somewhere...
Oh yes - of course...
Mildred Paltry.
"The Pink & Blue Screen"
well...
Stealing her ideas has to be easier than having my own!
hmm... growing up good... do be quiet... boys will be boys (ugh)... bad mothers, absent fathers ...grim, grim, grim... Grimm (hee hee)...
...incest, eroticism and rape?
eurgh!
as if we hadn't had enough of all THAT when we were doing soap operas!
KNOCK KNOCK
Come in!
AN IDEA IN A BOOK IS WORTH TWO IN THE HEAD
A SLEAZE CASTLE LOST TALE BY JEREMY DENNIS

Panda!
Oh, Honestly
what're you WEARING?
it's not like it's REAL gold!
You look like a Buck Rogers alien!
I do?!?
it'd be better if your HAIR was SILVER.
hm.
LOOK OUT! IT'S THE ALIEN QUEEN
So-what's up?
Jo-o-Pleease come shopping with me!
Panda - I have two broken legs, no money and tutorials to prepare!
but I'm going to Finnex!
They have LIFTS and I can LEND you money and GUESS what's in the BASEMENT?
Sigh
what.
um...
TOYS!
LOTS OF
Toys!
Toys?
well? are you COMING?
Toys! Toys!
realistic hair
posable limbs
it'd be research. for your thesis!
come on!
mf mf mm-mnt mfr tutorial!
Oh...
I don't know...
Tap Tap Tap
but I just want to SLEEEP!
zz
DINOSAUR BLISS
Too late!
well ler ah
REMEMBER RAGLAN SLEEVES?
Poo.

! gromp !
afternoon television is so boring.
bleh
bleh
blah blah
Z
INTO THE SOAP ZONE: JO'S DREAM
time to buy toys!
eeeeEEEEeeee
but HOW can I buy TOYS?
my FEET are STUCK in the mud?!
evil
heh heh heh
we're all FREEEEeeeeeee
TOYS
THUMP THUMP THUMP
BIG
BIG
BIG BEAST
I, MUD-RA, WILL FREE YOU FROM THE MUD!
NO!
erk eek sinking
why-why aren't you SINKING?
I, MUD RANGER WILL SAVE YOU WITH MY MUD POWERS!
THOMP THOMP
I CHOP CABBAGES!
bleb
Roar!
I'M NOT A CABBAGE!
oOOOOooooo
what pretty mud

KNOK
Z
KNOK smash tinkle KNOK
whuh?
buzz z buzz z z
eeeeeeeeee
HOT EIGHTIES FASHION!
& ENDANGERED MAMMALS
p-Panda?
isn't he sweet?
I knew you'd like it! It's one of those space aliens you like!
hee hee
a FAIR description, but...
I THINK it's an OTTER.
Oh? What's an otter?
late! late!
OH-
FOR HEAVEN'S sake!
an ENDANGERED MAMMAL.
what's "endangered?"
um... well...
IT'S TIME TO GET THINGS STARTED IT'S TIME TO LIGHT THE LIGHTS
What TIME is it? oh nooOOO!
7:30
what's wrong?
I spent all afternoon asleep!
So?
I have TUTORIALS TOMORROW!
horror
don't be silly!
You can prepare them at the last minute, as usual...
now LOOK what I've bought!
FINE

TALES FROM SLEAZE CASTLE

Gratuitous BUNNY COMIX

1

£1.30

T. Wiley & D. McKinnon

3 Birthdays

roar of the greasepaint

INTERLUDE : METAMOR

she was really bugging me

interlude : *walk the dog*

T. Wiley & D. McKinnon

www.ingramcontent.com/pod-product-compliance
Ingram Content Group UK Ltd.
Pitfield, Milton Keynes, MK11 3LW, UK
UKHW051126260726
13967UKWH00010B/2895

9 781905 692934